D0378684

owley, Joy.
hicken feathers /

2008.

a 12/17/08

With illustrations by David Elliot

PHILOMEL BOOKS

Patricia Lee Gauch, Editor

PHILOMEL BOOKS
A division of Penguin Young Readers Group.
Published by The Penguin Group.
Penguin Group (USA) Inc., 375 Hudson Street, New York, NY 10014, U.S.A.
Penguin Group (Canada), 90 Eglinton Avenue East, Suite 700, Toronto, Ontario M4P 2Y3, Canada (a division of Pearson Penguin Canada Inc.).
Penguin Books Ltd, 80 Strand, London WC2R 0RL, England.
Penguin Ireland, 25 St. Stephen's Green, Dublin 2, Ireland (a division of Penguin Books Ltd).
Penguin Group (Australia), 250 Camberwell Road, Camberwell, Victoria 3124, Australia (a division of Pearson Australia Group Pty Ltd).
Penguin Books India Pvt Ltd, 11 Community Centre, Panchsheel Park, New Delhi - 110 017, India.
Penguin Group (NZ), 67 Apollo Drive, Rosedale, North Shore 0632, New Zealand (a division of Pearson New Zealand Ltd.)
Penguin Books (South Africa) (Pty) Ltd, 24 Sturdee Avenue, Rosebank, Johannesburg 2196, South Africa.
Penguin Books Ltd, Registered Offices: 80 Strand, London WC2R 0RL, England.

Text copyright © 2008 by Joy Cowley. Illustrations copyright © 2008 by David Elliot. All rights reserved. This book, or parts thereof, may not be reproduced in any form without permission in writing from the publisher, Philomel Books, a division of Penguin Young Readers Group, 345 Hudson Street, New York, NY 10014. Philomel Books, Reg. U.S. Pat. & Tm. Off. The scanning, uploading and distribution of this book via the Internet or via any other means without the permission of the publisher is illegal and punishable by law. Please purchase only authorized electronic editions, and do not participate in or encourage electronic piracy of copyrighted materials. Your support of the author's rights is appreciated. The publisher does not have any control over and does not assume any responsibility for author or third-party websites or their content.
Published simultaneously in Canada.
Printed in the United States of America.
Design by Semadar Megged. The illustrations are rendered in.
Library of Congress Cataloging-in-Publication Data
Cowley, Joy. Chicken feathers / Joy Cowley ; with illustrations by David Elliot.
p. cm. Summary: Relates the story of the summer Josh spends while his mother is in the hospital awaiting the birth of his baby sister, and his pet chicken Semolina, who talks but only to him, is almost killed by a red fox. [1. Chickens—Fiction. 2. Pets—Fiction. 3. Farm life—Fiction. 4. Family life—Fiction.] I. Elliot, David, 1952– ill. II. Title.
PZ7.C8375Ch 2008 [Fic]—dc22 2007038635
ISBN 978-0-399-24791-0
10 9 8 7 6 5 4 3 2 1

THIS BOOK IS DEDICATED TO ELIZABETH MILLER, a gifted storyteller who has brought the magic of story to thousands of children. May she long continue to inspire the child in all of us.

The book is also for Tori, granddaughter of Dr. Maryann Manning. Tori was born while I was writing chapter nine, and she naturally found her place in the story.

Last but not least, it is for those marvelous birds who have invaded my life. There was Colonel Sanders, an old blind rooster who walked sideways toward me, guided by my voice, until he was leaning against my legs. When I picked him up and stroked his glossy black feathers, he cooed like a dove. There was Lily, a bantam hen who inhabited my studio. She laid her small eggs in the correspondence tray on my desk and interrupted my writing with triumphant egg songs. Beatrice the goose was devoted to us until she transferred her affections to an old woolly sheep. Ruby, a white Orpington hen, used to wait at the gate, rain or shine, for my return from town.

Pets may have a short life, but the love and wisdom they give us lasts an entire human span.

Chapter One

TUCKER AND ELIZABETH MILLER were serious about life. Maybe it was something to do with living on a farm with three thousand chickens, or maybe it was because their hearts were as soft as the new-laid eggs they took to market. Whatever, their son, Joshua, had a fair dose of that seriousness. When he did tell a joke, it was the kind that made folk groan and hold their stomachs as though they'd swal-

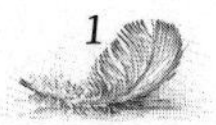

lowed ice cubes. Josh worried about things, not big things like earthquakes and tsunamis, but the little wrinkles in each day—how best to fix the lawn mower and who was doing the shopping for old Mrs. Waters, who broke her ankle falling off the horse she wasn't supposed to be riding. People said the Miller boy had a touch of softness to him—which is how Semolina came to be his pet.

Semolina was no ordinary chicken. She may have looked like any old hen, legs scaly with age, ragged tail feathers, comb pale and small, body on the plump side from sitting on the table beside Josh's plate. But it wasn't eating corn bread that made her unique. Fact was, Semolina could talk, really talk, and it started soon after the day Tucker Miller came up the path with the hen tucked under his arm.

"She's a character, this one," Tucker said to his son. "Too old to lay, fights with the other chickens. But I guess I don't have the heart to do the dirty. Josh, you're hankering for a pet. You want her?"

Josh, who was thinking along the lines of a puppy, nodded and carefully took the bird, who had the good sense not to peck his hand. Of course he knew Semolina. Who didn't?

If there were feathers flying in the barn, it was Semolina causing chaos. Chickens couldn't get to the drinking water because the old girl was there first, guarding it. Couldn't get heads down at the food trough, either—Semolina walked behind them, pulling out tail feathers. She was trouble with a capital *T*, and smart with it.

He lined an old wash basket with a blanket and set it on the front porch for her, but since his bedroom window

opened to the porch, it took no more than an hour or two for Semolina to decide that the head of Josh's iron bed was the best place to perch.

As for the talking, that began with a word here or there. "Josh," she'd cluck. "Josh, Josh. Josh." Then, "Food. Window. Hurry." Before long, she was chattering away like a picnic of parrots and then some. But the embarrassing thing was she'd only speak to Josh.

"She does so talk!" he told his parents. "Listen to this! Semolina, say it's a sunny day."

Semolina put her head on one side and stared with a blank yellow eye. "Caw-awk! Caw-awk!"

"Sunny day, Semolina! Sunny day!"

"Cawk!"

Tucker and Elizabeth smiled at each other, and Elizabeth kissed Josh on the top of his head the way she did when he was three years old. "Of course she talks," she said. "Sweet chicken talk."

The most serious matter in the Miller family concerned a sister or brother for Josh. Elizabeth Miller, nearly six months pregnant, ended up in the hospital on a Friday morning due

to something the doctor called complications. There was a danger she could lose the baby.

"What's wrong?" Josh asked.

Tucker pushed back his cap and scratched his head. "Blessed if I know. Your mom and I are not good layers, and that's the truth of it. We thought we'd be right this time."

Josh tried not to think about it. When he was six, he had sorted out his toys for a new baby that didn't come. "Lost it," people whispered, as though his mother had somehow forgotten where she'd put the baby. He never did play with those toys again. This time he wouldn't hope too much, so when disappointment came, he could tell himself it was what he expected.

If the baby wasn't complication enough, Saturday afternoon Semolina flew through Josh's window, landed beside his model yacht and demanded Grandma's brew from the cupboard in the laundry. The old hen had a wicked thirst for the brown water, as she called it. No one else liked the stuff. Grandma made it with hops and yeast in a big old tub at the back of her house, and Tucker reckoned it tasted as though she'd washed the socks of a baseball team in it. Grandma kept

giving it to Tucker. He stowed it in the cupboard behind the laundry powder and mousetraps, and there it stood, an army of large brown bottles with dusty shoulders and crown caps.

Saturday wasn't the first time Josh had gotten brew for Semolina. But it was the first time Tucker noticed that a bottle had been opened.

Josh felt bad. He wished his dad would get fired up like other fathers. He dang well hated the way Tucker looked at him soft-eyed as though he was going to cry.

"Dad?" he said. "I only took it for . . ."

But Tucker turned away without saying a word.

Josh wanted to explain. He'd given Grandma's brew to Semolina, fair trade for information about the missing eggs in the number-three henhouse. He wanted his father to believe that Semolina could really, truly, without-a-doubt talk.

But Tucker himself had his mouth closed thin. He just put the bottle in the trash can, his face as heavy as a rainy day, and sat on the porch swing, where he clasped and unclasped his bony hands and sighed so deep the air seemed to come from the soles of his feet.

Josh stomped into his room and threw himself on the

blue patchwork quilt. Semolina was in her usual place on the wrought iron bedpost. She fidgeted, and a reddish brown feather floated down to the pillow.

Josh glared at her. "What kind of hen drinks brew?"

"My kind, buddy." She snapped a yellow eye at him. "Ain't my fault you was caught."

She flopped from the bedpost to his bookcase, her claws scrabbling on the top shelf and upsetting a can of pencils. As she leaned against his picture of a three-masted sloop, Josh thought she looked mighty unsteady. "Talk to Dad, will you?" he begged. "Please? Just this once? Explain you made me get Grandma's brew."

She shook her wing feathers. "I told you umpteen times I ain't never wasting words on biggies. They got no ears for it. I made you do nothing, buddy. Fair trade, I said. Brown water for news about the fox."

Josh turned on his bed until his head was over the edge, his legs up the wall. "You got to tell him, Semolina. He thinks I drank it!"

"What a biggie dumb cluck!" she trilled. "One huff of your breath and he'd know it wasn't you."

Josh whirled around. In a quick, swooping movement he was on his feet, his hands outstretched. "I'll get him to smell *your* breath!" he cried. "That'll convince him!"

Semolina flew up in a frenzy of feathers, and Josh's fingers closed on air. Before he could open his hands again, that old fowl was out the window and onto the back porch, lurching across the boards, feathers ruffled.

"Come back!" Josh yelled.

She briefly turned her head. "Aw, shut your beak," she said as she disappeared into the garden.

• • •

The open bottle of brew had gone clean out of Tucker Miller's head by egg collection time. He had more important things to think about.

"Had a phone call from the doctor," he said as Josh climbed into the egg trailer. "They're keeping your mom in the hospital."

"Keeping her?" Josh frowned. His mother was never this sick. "Can't they fix what's wrong and send her home?"

"She could lose the baby—like those other times." Tucker started the tractor and yelled above the engine noise. "They reckon she'll be in the hospital till it's born." He put the tractor in gear, and his voice got swallowed up in the rattles as they rolled down the hill toward the barns. The trailer swung from side to side over ground as hard as nails. Most of the grass had dried and the wheels sent up dust behind them, like brown smoke.

Josh took off his shirt. This surely was the hottest day of all summer. The sun swam in a big blue bowl of sky, and shadows crouched small as though they were scared of get-

ting burned on the scorched earth. Days like this, his mother usually took him swimming in the river behind the woods. Josh counted weeks on his fingers. If babies took nine months to grow and his mother was six months pregnant, then he'd be back at school before she was home again. He wiped his shirt across his face. Spittin' bugs! He wanted a baby sister, sure, but there were limits to the cost.

His father stopped the tractor and swung his long legs down. "Okay, son. Back to the salt mines. Another day, another dollar."

He always said that.

Other chicken farmers had red barns, but Tucker Miller painted his inside and out with tar to keep the chickens free of parasites like lice and red mites. Since black was a color that sucked up heat, there were cooling systems in each of the nine big chicken houses.

"Yes, sir," Tucker had said to the reporter from the newspaper. "Our chickens are spoiled rich. Not only free range, they also have air-conditioning, cool in summer, and heaters to keep warm in winter. Take it from me, these hen hotels produce right royal eggs."

Josh thought that free range was a matter of opinion. The only chicken truly free was Semolina. The others were always kept inside the chicken houses but not in little cages. They could wander around, scratching in the straw, giving themselves dust baths, and when it was time to lay, they hopped up into one of a long line of nesting boxes and plopped out perfect little brown eggs. Well, mostly perfect. The eggs too small, too big or soft-shelled were sold cheap to Mr. Sorensen, who made wedding and birthday cakes.

Josh jumped off the trailer with a stack of egg baskets. "If she came home now, she could stay in bed—the same as in the hospital."

"Not the same. She's got a nurse checks her every four hours, and all the medicine right there—" Tucker took a load of baskets from Josh. "We're not taking any more risks, Josh. Not after trying seven years to get you a brother or sister."

"Did you try a long time to get me?"

"Yup." Tucker ruffled Josh's hair. "Some people are like that pesky chicken of yours—they just ain't good at laying. They got other talents."

"Semolina doesn't lay because she's old," Josh said.

"Right, son, and me and your mom ain't no spring chickens either. I reckon this'll be our last chance. Don't fret."

"Who's fretting?" Josh chewed the edge of his thumbnail. "It'd be okay to be a big brother, but I'm not holding my breath. I just want Mom home."

Tucker nodded. "That makes two of us. But I don't expect you to choke on pizza every night. We'll get someone in to cook regular meals and help with the house."

Josh shrugged. "It's okay, Dad. I like pizza."

Inside the first chicken house, sunlight melted dust and filled the air with gold. The floor was as busy as a city mall on Friday night. More than three hundred chickens scratched, clucked, pecked, fluffed in the straw in a haze that gave their feathers an orange glow. Josh closed the door and breathed in deep, the smell as thick as gravy. Everything about chickens, their feathers, feet, eggs, smelled like their poop. It was a rich smell, and Josh loved it. He wanted to believe that God had made people out of clay that smelled like chicken

poop, warm and friendly, full of good stuff for growth. His father said you could raise anything on chicken manure, and he would know. They sold the old chicken house straw by the truckload, and Tucker reckoned it made tomatoes as big as pumpkins.

Josh walked slow and light-footed lest he trod on something. The chickens were so used to him, they didn't get out of the way, and there were eggs hidden in the straw like Easter surprises. They got laid there when all the nesting boxes were full. Josh understood how that happened. Once when they had guests in the bathrooms, he had to go under

a tree in the backyard and hope no one was watching. You couldn't expect a chicken to hold off when an egg was coming into the world.

He found twenty-seven good eggs in the straw and two that were broken.

The morning Elizabeth was admitted to the hospital, Josh had sat on the swing seat on the back porch, Semolina beside him. He told Semolina how scary it was seeing his mom in bed with a needle in the back of her hand, a long tube joining her to a bag of fluid.

"So you took her to the vet," Semolina said.

"Animals and birds have vets," Josh said. "Human beings have doctors."

Semolina did not like to be corrected. "Excuse me. I forgot to tell you I know the difference between biggies and chickens. So your mom's gone broody. That's natural, buddy."

He tried to explain without offending her. "The baby's not due until September. If it comes now, it'll die."

Semolina's mood changed. She hopped onto his knee, her claws sharp through his jeans, and clacked her beak. "Aw, aw," she crooned.

Josh felt his eyes become hot. "They'll be heartbroken if they lose it."

Step by step, the old hen crawled up his shirt until she was resting her beak on his shoulder. Her feathers quivered as a sigh went through her. "Eggs is easier," she said. "They only take three weeks to hatch."

While Josh went through the barns searching for the eggs that had been laid on the straw, Tucker did the nest boxes from outside, lifting up the lids, filling his baskets, cleaning out the occasional blob of gray-and-white poop.

"The water all right?" he asked Josh.

Josh nodded. Each of the nine chicken houses had two fresh water fountains that had to be checked daily. "No problems," he said as he put the last lot of eggs in the trailer. "How was number three today?"

In answer, Tucker scrunched up his mouth and shoulders. That meant the egg count in the number-three shed was still down.

"How much?"

"Same. Three to four dozen missing."

Josh said carefully, "You don't think it could be a fox?"

Tucker frowned. "How would a fox get in?"

Josh was stuck. Any mention of a talking chicken would send his dad into a silence colder than snow.

"I—I just thought—it might be a fox."

Tucker said, "Ain't been a fox here in years. Anyways, foxes come at night. Chickens lay in the morning. Even if a fox did find a way in, which is downright impossible, the timing's all wrong, and what makes you think a fox would prefer eggs to chicken? You ever consider that?"

Josh was silent. Maybe Semolina lied about the fox to get brew. That was unlikely but possible.

A long breath went out of Tucker, and his shoulders dropped. He put his hand on Josh's head. "Sorry, son. When a man's got worries, his jaw can get snappier than a turtle's.

Come on. Let's get this lot down to the sorting shed. We need to get ourselves cleaned up before visiting hour."

Elizabeth Miller had a room of her own in the hospital and a bed that was bent like a V, with the bottom part steeper than the top. Josh ran to her, the toes of his shoes squeaking on the smooth floor. As he hugged her, he asked, "Doesn't all your blood flow up to your head?"

She laughed and tickled him under the arms. "It might improve my brain."

He laughed. "Mom, your brain couldn't get improved. It's a best-Mom-in-the-world super-brain!" He put his head on the pillow beside her. "What about the baby?"

"I guess she's getting her share. I can feel her wriggling. Want to feel?" She grabbed his hand and held it on her stomach, but all he could feel was the rise and fall of his mom's breathing.

He sat beside her, took some grapes out of a paper sack and put them in the white fruit bowl on her nightstand.

Nearly everything in the room was white, but Elizabeth Miller shone with color—skin like polished wood, dark red hair, pink cheeks, brown eyes. She looked like the magazine ad for Dr. Granger's Elixir of Life, good for everything from sore feet to earwax. "Do you really have to stay here until the baby's born?"

"Oh, honey, I hope not. But if it has to be that way, we'll cope. Won't we?"

He nodded. "Sure."

"It'll be worth it," she said. "When the baby's here, you'll forget about the long wait and I'll forget that I lay in the hospital bored out of my skull. Tell me about your day. Have you been working on your boat?"

"Not much time. I'll get back to it."

"You like the motor Daddy bought you?"

"It hasn't come yet. We figured maybe a week or two before we pick it up. I promised Annalee first ride on the river. That okay?"

"You mean I've lost first ride to pretty little Annalee Binochette?" She laughed and pushed her fingers through his hair. This hair ruffling was something both his parents did to

him, but Mom's touch on his scalp made his eyelids drop like heavy blinds. He curled up beside her.

"What has that sassy Semolina been up to?" she asked.

The chicken barns had been long silent when Semolina tottered into Josh's room.

"You're late," he said.

She spread her wings and with great effort flapped to the back of his chair. She looked poorly. Her feathers were rumpled. Her comb was extra pale. "You spilled the beans on the fox?" she said.

He was still mad at her. "My dad didn't believe me!"

"It is a fox," she insisted.

"Dad says number one, there are no foxes, and number two, chickens don't talk. So you tell him! Semolina, I've begged you till I'm blue in the face. You got to say something to my father!"

She hunched down and closed her eyes but a few seconds later opened them. "Water! I need water."

Josh got out of bed and went to the bathroom. He put his

blue mug under the cold tap, came back and held it in front of her. She dipped her beak in, lifted her head and swallowed again and again, the small feathers at her throat fluttering with every sip. When she had finished, he put the mug down on the chair and climbed back into bed.

She was restless. "Aw, this headache's bad," she moaned.

Josh pulled the sheet around his ears. "That's what happens to chickens when they drink brew," he said.

Chapter Two

IF YOU LOOKED AT THE MILLER farm from a distance, you'd be hard-pressed to tell what they raised on it. It was just a big patch of dirt with a house, nine big black barns, a flat-roofed concrete barn nearby, a tractor shed and a green patch of Swiss chard out back. But turning in the gate, you'd know those big black barns were full of chickens. The crooning noise and the warm smell would soon tell you. Now, the

Binochette farm next door, there was no doubt about that. Strangers could pick it out half a mile away, a dairy farm with green fields along a riverbank, big black-and-white cows up to their hocks in grass and rolls of hay plastic-wrapped like giant salamis. Everything about the Binochettes' place was tidy. From that half-mile view it looked like a toy cow farm with its fresh-painted barns and picket fences.

Tucker's mother-in-law always commented, and today was no different. On the way back from the train station, as Tucker drove around that curve in the road, she called out from her seat, "Stop! Stop right here!" Tucker pulled over, the car brushing sun-dried grasses and disturbing small blue and yellow butterflies. Grandma lowered her window. She smiled down on the black-and-white cows, the neat fences, the long swoop of the Grayhawk River. "Now that's what I call a farm."

In the seat beside her, Josh felt the sting of unsaid words. He wanted to lean toward her and shout in her good ear, "Pardon me, Grandma, our farm doesn't have the river for irrigation or hired hands to make pretty picket fences, but we have happy chickens. Yes, ma'am. The Miller chickens

are equally happy and healthy as those Hereford cows, and if you look past the Binochettes' farm, past the black barns and dust, you'll see a dark green field of Swiss chard that gets watered nearly every day. I know because I turn on the sprinklers, and you won't get better Swiss chard anywhere. That's what gives our famous eggs their rich yellow yolks that people like to see with their bacon and hash browns."

Of course, he didn't say a word. He sat in the backseat

as still as a rock, sharing his father's silence, while the heat poured through Grandma's open window and the blue and yellow butterflies flew back into shade in the long grass.

When Tucker told him Grandma was coming to keep house for them, Josh had been half pleased, half afraid, and he hadn't known which half was which. Now he remembered. One half was about her pickiness, the way she criticized everything, and the other concerned her cooking. She could do suppers a hundred delicious ways, and her peach pies were even better than the peach pies made by his mom, who had the same recipe. He promised himself he would think of Grandma's cooking every time she got picky. That seemed only fair.

Grandma looked like a cook. She was a widely spaced woman, different from her daughter, who was tall and lean, and it always seemed strange to Josh that a grandmother could have young skin matched up with old hair. From where he sat, the side of her face was as smooth as sanded wood while her pinned-up hair was like a heap of snow.

Without a word, Tucker rolled up the window from his side and steered the car back onto the road.

"How's their little girl?" Grandma asked. "Annabel Whosamecallit."

"Annalee Binochette," Josh said loudly. "She's not little, Grandma. She's fourteen and grown—" He stopped, unable to describe the changes in Annalee. Last summer she wasn't much bigger than he was, and they climbed trees together in the woods at the back of the farm. This summer she didn't climb trees. She was tall and had bumps in her T-shirt, but that wasn't all. Her ears were pierced, she wore bright pink nail polish and there was a silver ring on one of her toes. When she said a boy named Bob had given her the toe ring, Josh had felt a creeping sadness. His friend Annalee was leaving him for a world that seemed uncomfortably distant.

Tucker smiled. "She's working for us this summer. Vacation job, sorting eggs two days a week."

"Pretty little thing," said Grandma. "A younger child too, isn't there? Handsome, that entire family."

Josh grunted. Annalee's brother, Harrison, was only nine but in the same year at school as Josh and the smartest kid in the class, something Josh didn't want to think about too much. Not that he had much choice. Harrison reminded him

often enough. "Need help with your homework, Slosh?" he'd say.

He tried to ignore Harrison, which wasn't easy, especially with Elizabeth at him to play with that nice little Binochette boy. "Maybe he's difficult because he feels left out," Elizabeth had said.

"Mom, he's left out because he's difficult," Josh argued. "He's downright mean."

"The way to get rid of your enemies is to make them your friends." Elizabeth almost sang it like a line from a hymn.

Josh stopped trying to explain. Harrison Binochette wasn't an enemy. He wasn't anything except Annalee's little brother with the first *r* left out.

"You're blessed to have such nice neighbors, Tucker," Grandma said. "Did you hear me, Tucker? What's with the face? Cheer up. Elizabeth's as strong as a horse. I got you some more of my brew."

Tucker took the suitcases up the stairs while Grandma stood on the porch fanning herself with a magazine from her

knitting bag. She was looking over the chicken farm, eyes as dark as peppercorns, noting changes since her last visit. Josh suspected she was making a mental list of suggestions that would come out later. He followed her gaze and saw the dried lawn going bald, the dangling wire on the clothesline, clothespins spilled on the ground, dirt and dead leaves on the porch, an assortment of dusty shoes and boots kicked off at the door.

"We've been awful busy," he said.

There was no way of knowing if she'd heard. Her face shone with heat, and there were wet patches under the arms of her brown dress. The magazine flapped back and forth, creating more noise than breeze. It was a book about babies' clothes, with a cover picture of a baby without teeth.

She saw him looking and stopped fanning herself. "From the way things are around here, there won't be much time for knitting. What's Elizabeth doing?"

"Huh?"

"In the hospital. Lying in bed. Is she knitting for the baby? I don't think so. Knowing my daughter, she'll be reading. Books, books, books. Someone's got to knit for the poor

little thing." She took a deep breath, raising and lowering her sweaty arms. "I made you silk and wool vests before you were born, wool sweaters, booties. I knitted you a wool shawl so fine it could pass through a wedding ring." She looked hard at him, then put the magazine back in her bag. "Natural fibers," she said. "All natural, remember that."

Tucker clattered down the stairs calling, "Your room's ready, Augusta. I turned on the fan."

She heard him and went in the door. "First things first," she said as she walked toward the kitchen.

Josh knew the kitchen was tidy. He and his father had spent an hour yesterday cleaning and sweeping. Tucker had hauled a blue-checked tablecloth out of the laundry and ironed it. Josh had picked some of those red flowers out front for the glass vase. Grandma would find nothing wrong with the kitchen.

Big mistake, he discovered. Semolina was the thing that was wrong. Not that his hen had done anything terrible. She was simply sitting on the table as usual, waiting for lunch, her tail feathers spread over his bread plate. But with them being late and all, the tablecloth was a bit wrinkled and the

flowers had been pulled out of the vase. She'd probably tried to eat them.

"You've still got that scrawny chicken!" Grandma shrieked, waving her bag. "Out! Out!"

Semolina shifted sideways, fixing a wary eye on the old woman.

"Off the table!" cried Grandma, and *whump*, the knitting bag caught Semolina on her side, sending her clean over the top of a chair and onto the floor. She landed on her feet, wings spread, and ran out of the kitchen, her claws scrabbling and sliding on the polished wood.

"She's housebroken!" Josh yelled. "She's very clean." He went after her, but by the time he got to the door, she had disappeared under the porch in a huff of feathers. He went back into the kitchen. "Semolina always sits on the table at mealtimes. I feed her!"

Grandma was opening and shutting drawers. "This is a chicken farm, and chickens have their place. I'll bet the Whosamecallits next door don't have a cow sitting on their kitchen table. Aha! So that's where Elizabeth keeps the aprons."

Josh was torn between defending his pet to Grandma and crawling under the house to see if Semolina was all right. "A cow can't sit on a table," he said. "The table would fall down or there'd be no room for the food or both. You hardly notice a chicken."

His grandmother put the apron over her head and turned her back to him. "Fasten these for me, there's a good boy," she said, holding out the apron ties. "I'll fix us ham-and-corn fritters for lunch—with a Caesar salad. You can set the table if you like. Only remember, if that chicken comes into this kitchen one more time, it's gravy."

. . .

Semolina wedged herself in the narrowest place under the house, where Josh couldn't reach her. He could see her, but she refused to look at him. She crouched with her head bent, one eye focused on the ground while the other inspected the gaps in the floorboards.

"Aw, come out!" he said. "It wasn't all that bad."

Her head twitched slightly, but she didn't answer.

"You haven't had lunch," he said. "Look, I got you a corn-and-ham fritter."

Even that didn't work.

"You going dumb on me, Semolina?" He wiped cobwebs away from his face. Lying on his belly in the dust under the house was not Josh's favorite thing, and besides, Annalee would be over at two o'clock to sort the eggs. She might even be there now. He unwrapped the corn-and-ham fritter and left it lying on the paper napkin. "Suit yourself. When you get over it, I'll be in the sorting barn."

Chapter Three

BECAUSE THE EGGS HAD TO be kept at a temperature under seventy degrees, the sorting barn was always cool, and Annalee's arms were dotted with shivery spots she called chicken flesh. Today she was wearing a pink T-shirt with *I love Paris* in gold letters across her chest. He read it more slowly than was necessary and then, in case she'd noticed, he asked, "Does that gold stuff come off in the washing machine?"

She shrugged the question away. "I heard about your mom. Is she—I mean the baby . . . Are they going to be okay?"

"Yeah, the doctors think so. But she has to stay in the hospital a real long time."

"I know. Your grandma called my mother."

Phone calls already? He stepped up beside Annalee to help with the eggs and to breathe in the flower smell of her shampoo. Today her hair was tied back with a ribbon. "Until the baby's born," he said. "Three whole months."

She nodded, her arms moving across each other in an easy rhythm, separating large- and small-grade eggs and slotting each into spaces in the cardboard trays. "How's your boat?" she asked.

"Haven't had time to work on it, but now that Grandma's here, I reckon I'll finish it. I've got the engine."

"Really?"

"Yep. Nearly new Johnson. It gets here in two weeks."

"Cool!" Annalee's smile was like an explosion. "Remember you promised me a ride on the river."

"Sure thing." He stood taller so that his eyes were in line with the freckles on her nose. "You still want to go fishing?"

"Josh, that would be so neat! How come you already got a motor?"

"Dad did it for me. He fixed it—part of my wages."

She paused, an egg in each hand. "So when will you be able to go fishing?"

"Soon. Next month, maybe." His eyes slid sideways to *I love Paris*, and he wondered how come girls grew up so

quick. She looked better now than she did last year, but he preferred last summer's Annalee Binochette. He couldn't imagine those long pink fingernails scooping up mud to throw at him.

"That will be so exciting," she said. "I told Bob about your skiff. He was extra interested—I mean really intense. Do you mind if he comes to see it?"

Bob. That was the guy in her class who'd given her the silver toe ring. She was wearing it again today. It poked out the front of her right sandal like a dog collar on her second toe.

Josh didn't know what to say. He watched her busy with eggs, her hands moving fast, picking up, crossing over, up, down, like a piano player.

"Bob said he's going to build a boat too. Maybe you could give him some tips."

The silence went on too long. Josh could hear his heartbeat in his ears. He turned toward the door. "What was that?"

"What was what?"

"Scratching noise, sort of. Might be that old Semolina." He went over, turned the door handle and put his head out.

"Nah. Not her. She must still be under the house in a sulking fit. Grandma whopped her on the tail feathers, lunchtime."

"No!" Annalee's face creased in sympathy.

"Not real hard," he said quickly. "More about hurt feelings, I guess. She won't talk to me."

"Your grandmother won't talk to you? Why?"

"Not her. Semolina."

"Oh. Yes. I forgot." Annalee's eyes went all careful, and she turned back to the egg crates.

Josh had seen his parents exchange that same look. "You said you believed me."

Annalee frowned. "Josh, I—I do believe. I believe that you really, truly think Semolina talks to you."

"But not that she talks."

"I didn't say that. It's just—well, chickens don't. They can't."

"Yes, they can!" he cried. "Parrots can. Budgies. Ravens."

"Not chickens. And not like you say—" Annalee's face was scrunched up into lines of effort. "Semolina is very smart and I think she's special, but—let's not discuss this, Josh."

"I told you," Josh said. "She started just like a parrot. A few words. Then more. But not to other people. There are parrots who only speak to their owners. I read that somewhere."

Annalee whirled around. Her face smoothed out, and her eyes widened. "It's there again!"

"What?"

"The scratching on the door—only I think it's more a tapping."

Josh heard it too. That crazy old Semolina was turning his lie into the truth. He opened the door and saw her crouched on the top step as though she were laying an egg. "So you changed your mind," he said. "Okay. Come in, and hurry. It's hot outside."

She stood up, shook herself, and small puffs of dust rose from her feathers. Then, taking her time, she arched her feet over the step and onto the floor. She didn't look at Josh. A few more steps and she flew up to the sorting bench to sit beside Annalee.

Josh laughed. "I don't know why she's still mad at me. It was Grandma who knocked her off the table."

The membranes closed over Semolina's eyes as fast as a camera shutter.

"Poor Semolina!" Annalee raised pink pointed fingers and stroked the reddish brown feathers from head to neck to back. "I hope she wasn't hurt."

Semolina opened her beak and made a soft cawing noise like a dove.

"She likes me," Annalee said.

"Of course she does. If she didn't like you so much, she wouldn't poke her beak in here. She's gotten very political about it."

Annalee had turned her hand over so that the backs of her nails combed the chicken's feathers. "You mean, the eggs?"

"Uh-huh. You know how she describes us eating eggs? Murder. Don't ask me how she got a word like *murder*. I told her eggs don't turn into chickens if they aren't fertile. So she goes on about roosters too, how biggies kill all newly hatched roosters."

"Biggies?"

"That's what she calls human beings, remember? She thinks people are cruel monsters. I told her most slugs and

snails think chickens are evil. She doesn't take notice. Semolina can never bear to lose an argument—" Josh stopped. Annalee's face was a closed door and her fingers, trailing over Semolina's wing tips, were slow and without direction.

The Annalee of last year had believed him. She had wanted him to repeat every word Semolina said, and once, on the porch swing, she begged the old hen to talk to her too. But a year away at school had changed more than her body—it had done something to her mind as well. Now he sometimes felt that he and Annalee were living on different planets. He picked up Semolina and put her on the floor. "We'd better get these eggs done," he said.

Annalee looked sideways at him. "I'm sorry, Josh."

"It's okay."

"You're my friend. Semolina's my friend."

"I know." But the truth of it was he didn't know. He pulled down some empty cartons from the top shelf and moved farther down the bench.

Suddenly Annalee squealed and jumped backward. Then she laughed with her hand over her mouth. "Semolina! Oh, Josh, she just picked at my toe ring."

Semolina advanced, wings spread, neck stretched low to the ground, eye fixed on the shining silver bar behind the pink toenail. But Annalee was too quick. She pulled her foot back. The old hen paused, and in that instant, Josh grabbed her. "Semolina, that's not nice!"

"She likes it!" Annalee cried. "Look at her. She can't take her eyes off it."

"It's shiny, that's why."

Then Annalee did an amazing thing. She drew her knee up to her chin and said, "She can have it. It'll be Lady Semolina's leg ring." With that she slid the band of silver off her toe, and Josh saw that it wasn't a ring at all but a thin strip of metal bent almost in a circle. It could fit any size. Annalee held it toward Josh. "Lift her up and I'll put it on her."

"You sure?"

"Sure, I'm sure." Gently, Annalee bent the silver around Semolina's scaly right leg. When she let it go, the ring fell down to the top of the foot and hung like a bracelet. Annalee laughed. "It looks so elegant!"

"But it's yours," said Josh. "He—someone gave it to you."

"Oh, Bob won't mind. Put her down, Josh. Let's see how it looks when she walks."

Josh expected Semolina to peck at it and make a fuss, but she didn't. She walked across the sorting shed floor with her head bent, foot lifted high.

"What do you think of that?" Josh asked her.

"Cool!" said Semolina.

It had happened. Semolina had talked. He looked at Annalee, whose eyes were wide with shock. "Did you hear that?" he asked.

"She said—cool!"

"Yeah. She forgot herself. Well done, Semolina. Now say thank you to Annalee."

Semolina raised the ringed foot and put it down again.

"Say something else," Josh insisted.

Annalee crouched in front of the hen. "Say *cool* again. Please?"

Semolina blinked. "Caw. Caw-caw-caw."

"Oh." Annalee stood up. "My mistake. It was just a chicken noise."

"No, it wasn't! She said *cool*, and then she said *caw* to cover up *her* mistake. That's the truth, isn't it, Semolina?" Josh waited, but the cunning old bird wasn't saying a word. That did it for Josh. He picked her up, carried her to the door like an old feather duster and set her on the ground. "Go back to the house and talk to Grandma," he said.

Softly, in a hen noise the size of a whisper, she said, "Aw, shut your beak," and stalked off, jingling the silver ring on her right leg.

Chapter Four

NO ONE COULD EXPLAIN WHY a boy raised on a chicken farm, hundreds of miles from the sea, was so fascinated by boats. Josh couldn't explain it himself. While other toddlers wheeled plastic cars across the carpet chanting, "Brrrm, brrm!" Josh had climbed on a chair and sailed his drinking cup around the kitchen sink. When he was four, Tucker took

him down to the Grayhawk River at the back of the Binochettes' farm and together they made boats from folded magazine pages to sail on a slow brown current that sucked and swallowed their little paper craft. Even then Josh wanted to make a boat that wouldn't sink.

He collected pictures of ships, everything from Spanish galleons and Chinese junks to oceangoing liners, and for the bathtub, he made toy boats with propellers powered by twisted rubber bands.

Last winter, Tucker and Elizabeth had promised to drive him clear across five states to the California coast, where waves crashed on white sand beaches and boats sat side by side in huge parking lots called marinas. That was before the baby began.

"Don't worry. We'll do it as soon as the baby's big enough to travel," promised Tucker. "We'll take a boat trip to Catalina Island and you can swim with those seeing glasses, taste the salt. It's a different world under the ocean."

"He's already tasted the sea." Elizabeth smiled.

"When?" said Josh. "I don't remember."

Elizabeth put her hand on her stomach. "Before a baby's

born, it swims in a little sea inside its mother. It's called amniotic fluid. The little sea is salty just like the big sea."

"How did I breathe in it?" Josh asked.

"You didn't," she replied. "Babies breathe when they leave the little sea for the dry land. But they remember the little sea. The salt is in their blood. It's in their tears."

Tucker drummed his fingers on the table. "Next year, California. This year, son, you'll build a real boat."

Josh sat bolt upright. "Spittin' bugs, Dad! You mean that? What kind of boat?"

"Oh, I dunno. I reckon a skiff like in those old *Popular Mechanics* magazines, beechwood frame, double-skin ply. You can paddle it on the river. Might even get a little outboard motor, go upstream fishing." Tucker laughed his long slow laugh. "I guess building a boat will take about as long as building a baby, and it'll be just as much a blessed miracle."

Josh's boat grew in the tractor shed. The skiff was eight feet long and nearly three feet wide, with a shallow V bottom and flotation blocks under the seats in the bow and stern.

Tucker had helped Josh cut the frames from laminated beech wood and shown him how to steam ply panels for the hull over the old boiler. The panels, warm and wet, bent easily along the curves of the frame, nesting tight against the keel. Tucker fastened the ply covering with bronze screws that wouldn't rust no how, no way. After that, though, Josh did all the work himself, with his father keeping an eye on things by pretending he needed to come into the shed for tools.

When egg sorting was over, Josh worked on his boat. The skiff was upside down on the concrete floor and Josh was caulking the plywood joins when Semolina waddled in, the silver ring glinting on her right foot. She walked right up to the can of caulking cement.

"Watch that stuff," Josh said, pointing with his knife. "It sets hard as rock. Dip your beak in that and you'll never open it again."

She shifted to a safe distance and pulled her head in against her body.

"I was only joking," Josh said. "You still mad at me on

account of Grandma? That's not my doing. Grandma is Grandma. You know, she's not as crabby as she looks. You can still come in my window."

Semolina hopped onto a drum of engine oil and became busy pecking an itch under her wing feathers.

"You got nothing to say?" Josh shrugged and went back to spreading the paste over the plywood seams. If he didn't do a good job on this, the gaps would become leaks. With the putty knife he eased the paste into the cracks. He glanced up at Semolina. "I never knew a chicken so moody. What's wrong with you?"

For answer, Semolina's claws rattled on the oil drum as she turned her back to him.

"Aw, come on, Semolina. Who are you mad at? Grandma? Me? Or yourself? You talked in front of Annalee. The silver ring did it. You forgot, didn't you?"

Semolina groomed the feathers under the other wing.

"You could have said more. With Mom and Dad, I get your point, but Annalee? Put yourself in my shoes. It's bug-spittin' embarrassing her thinking I make it up. You like Annalee, so what's the problem?"

She did an all-over feather shake that sounded like a shower of hail. Then she stretched her neck toward the boat and said, "That thing going on Grayhawk River?"

"Yep."

"Where?"

"The back of Annalee's place. It'll fit on Dad's trailer. Me and Annalee are going upriver to fish, and don't worry, you're not invited."

She clacked her beak in disapproval. "Water ain't natural—except for drinking." She paused and clucked twice, a cooing sound. "The brown kind," she said hopefully.

"No!" Josh pointed his caulking knife at her. "No more brew."

"I got extra news for you."

"Semolina! I can't. That's definite. Good-bye apple pie. Hard cheer, no brew."

"What's with the apple pie?"

"I don't know. I made it up. I'm just trying to tell you, Semolina. I couldn't get you brown water if I tried."

She fixed him with a yellow eye. "The fox is wanting more eggs."

"You're kidding!" He sat back on his heels. "More?"

"That's what I said, buddy. He's got a racket going with raccoons, rats, ferrets, some bears. Maybe not the bears. Those girls in house three like a good story. But the old fox wanting more eggs, that's no story. If they don't deliver, then he switches to eating chickens, quick as a blink. Better tell your father."

"Semolina, my father is definite there hasn't been a fox around these parts for years. He thinks I'm making it up. You talk to him! He's a nice guy. If he catches that old fox, he'll serve you Grandma's brew for the rest of your days."

"No."

"Semolina, please! Give me a break!"

She turned her head away.

"I can get you ginger ale, lemonade, cold tea with lemon. Look, I bring you Grandma's pancakes, don't I? You had the bowl of leftover whipped cream." He scooped up some more caulking cement. "Dad says no way can the fox get those eggs."

"There's a hole," she said.

He shook his head. "No hole. I been over the number-

three chicken house about a hundred times and there's no hole for a fox to get in."

"There is a hole," she repeated.

"Tell me where," he demanded.

Slowly, she turned to face him. "I'll tell you when you get me brown water."

"Semolina, you drive me crazy!" He put down the putty knife and held out his hands to her.

She flew from the oil drum and collided with his chest, knowing that he would catch her. He scratched the back of her neck as she settled her head against his neck. "You are one terrible old bird," he said. "What am I going to do with you?"

"Brown water," she replied.

When Grandma went with them on hospital visits, Josh and his dad didn't get much talking space. Grandma took over her daughter, telling her how to look after herself, what to say to the doctors and nurses, what she should be doing for the baby.

"Be positive, Elizabeth. Don't even think of popping it out."

"I don't," said Elizabeth.

"What we believe will be our reality, Elizabeth. Strong thoughts make a strong child. No room for any of your slippy-sloppy fatalistic stuff."

"Yes, Mother." Elizabeth Miller smiled and reached out to ruffle Josh's hair.

"Your problem always, Elizabeth, is you get too easily discouraged," Grandma said. "As a child you bent every which way the wind blew. You didn't get that from my side of the family."

"No, Mother."

Grandma reached into her knitting bag and pulled out a tiny knitted coat. "Green suits a girl or a boy. Natural fibers, Elizabeth. Pure wool off a sheep's back. I've always thought it a shame I could never teach you how to knit."

Later that day, when Josh and Tucker were putting grain into the chicken feeders, Josh said, "Why is Grandma like that?"

"Like what, son?"

"So picky, so scratchy mean to Mom."

Tucker spread a rain of yellow wheat off the end of his shovel and dust danced in the sunlight. "She ain't mean, Josh. She loves your mother to pieces, but she's never let go of the little girl that was once hers. Elizabeth knows and she takes it all kindly."

Josh had a small shovel with a cutoff handle, but he worked as hard as Tucker, the muscles on his arms moving like snakes. "I wish she'd be, you know, nice."

"Nice comes in all shapes and sizes," said Tucker. "Your grandma's got a good heart, bless her, but she worries too much. That's the way of picky people. They need lots of love to make them stop picking on others. Bible says so."

"Does it?"

"Well, if it doesn't, it should. Your grandma's been mighty lonely since Grandpa died. You could pass more time with her. She'd like that."

Josh was silent. It wasn't easy to sit with a grandmother who wiped a toothpaste smudge off the corner of your mouth with a spit-wet handkerchief and looked in your ears to see if you washed.

Tucker emptied another sack of wheat into the trailer. "Price of wheat's gone up, egg count down again—the teeter-totter of economics, Josh."

"Number-three house?"

"Yup. Way down yesterday. Only fourteen dozen eggs. It's not easy, son. Insurance don't pay all the hospital either. We should be down-on-our-knees grateful your grandma's working here for nothing."

Wheat dust filled Josh's nose and throat, and he coughed. "Dad, you're sure it's not a fox getting the eggs? What if it was really a fox, and maybe raccoons and other critters?"

Tucker had heard Josh's fox theory so often, he would not waste more breath on it. He pushed his shovel into the mound of wheat on the trailer. "I just reminded myself. Yesterday Annalee went home without her pay. You mind running over to the Binochettes' when you finish here?"

Josh agreed a mite too quickly. His father looked up and smiled. "Didn't think it'd be any hardship," he said.

Grandma was one of those worry wrinkles that Josh couldn't quite straighten out. He knew she thought the Binochette family was up there with the president and the Queen of England. She would have jumped at a chance to go to the Binochette farm with him, but he deliberately didn't ask her. I'll make up for it, he promised himself. I'll help her with supper. I'll do the dishes. He tucked the pay envelope into the pocket of his overalls and made off, lickety-split, past the chicken houses, through the fence and over green fields of

summer grass. He had long legs like his father, but he went so fast they were shaky by the time he got to the Binochettes' front porch. Annalee and Harrison were sitting on the step with playing cards spread around them. Josh stopped on the path and bent over, hands on his knees, to get his breath back.

"Hi, Splosh," said Harrison. "Two aces, a king and a queen. Beat that."

Annalee stood up and swept her hair back. It was hanging loose on her shoulders like a black waterfall. "Is something wrong?" she asked.

"No." He felt in his pocket. "Dad said he didn't give you your pay."

"Oh, that."

She walked toward him, and again he inhaled the mist of flowers that seemed to hang around her hair. It made him aware that his clothes were steeped in chicken smell and wheat dust.

"I could have gotten it next week," she said.

Harrison had scooped up the cards and was shuffling them awkwardly, dropping them between his fingers. Josh

was pleased to see his clumsiness, and then he felt bad for being pleased.

Harrison smiled up at him. "Now she can buy a new dress to go out with her boyfriend."

Josh didn't say anything. He could shuffle cards when he was only seven. He never dropped them. For a while he stood on the path in front of Annalee, who had the pay envelope squished between two hands as though she didn't know what to say either. Then he nodded, the way his father sometimes did, and turned to walk away.

It was Harrison who called out. "Hey, Splosh! Guess what I saw yesterday. In the woods at the back of your place! A great big red fox!"

Wang-a-dang! Now there was proof! Harrison Binochette had seen the fox with his very own eyes. Josh ran back home, lit up with excitement, tingling to tell his father he'd been right all along. But the only person around was Grandma, and she was not impressed.

"Fox? That's nothing. We had wolves in our woods. Big and mean. You could hear them howling from one hilltop to another. Found wolf bones in a cave once. Bear got it. You washed your hands? Go and scrub up and make a job of it. You can set the table."

The light inside him went out. He looked at his hands. "Sure, Grandma."

"I hope you're hungry, Joshua. It's a good one tonight. Those cornmeal hush puppies you like and catfish in beer batter."

"Beer batter?" He looked at her. "Made with your brew?"

"Best batter there is," she said. "Don't worry. Cooking drives off the alcohol. No kid gets drunk on my fried fish."

Beer batter, he thought. Brew, fox, hole, eggs. He headed for the door. "How long will supper be, Grandma?"

"About as long as a piece of string. Don't you forget that table!"

"Right now, Grandma," he said, and he went outside to find Semolina.

Chapter Five

CAULKING CEMENT HAD DRIED on Josh's hands, and the only way to get it off was with a file from the tractor tool kit. He sat on the oil drum in the fading light, trying to see the difference between cement and skin. The setting sun shone through the poplars, touched the chicken houses with patches of fire and painted an orange glow on the floor of the tractor shed. "People still go around the world by sail," he

said to Semolina, who was crouched at his feet. "I want to do that one day."

"I ain't going with you, buddy," she said, wiping her beak on his shoe. With some effort she stood up and tottered over to the old cracked cup without a handle. It sat on the floor, empty. She let out a sound that was as close to a chicken sigh as he'd heard, then she used one of her longer words. "Pathetic!"

"Sorry. Grandma's catfish batter took most of the bottle. I only got what was left." He rubbed his hands together. They sounded like sandpaper. "Folk say when the sun sets over the sea, there's a green flash on the horizon."

"Ain't so," said Semolina. "Tarkah never lays her eggs over the sea. You ever see a chicken lay in water?"

Josh laughed and slid down to the concrete floor. He patted his shirt, and the old hen waddled over and settled against his chest. He could feel her warmth, her heartbeat inches away from his own, and smell the brew on her breath. "I haven't heard those Tarkah stories in the longest time," he said. "Tell me again."

A veil of skin closed over her eyes, as though she was

dreaming. "Tarkah is the first chicken, the mother of all the universe. One by one, she laid every star in the sky."

"You're talking about God," said Josh.

"Yeah. You got it, buddy."

"But God isn't a chicken," Josh argued.

"She is to chickens." Semolina turned her head and unveiled a yellow eye. "You want me to tell this story or what?"

"Go on."

"The earth egg was a real goodie. So Tarkah said, 'This egg will grow all my family.' So she sat on the earth egg for thousands of years until the mountains cracked and out flew birds of all kinds, eagles, sparrows, owls. But her favorite birds were the chickens."

"What about people?" Josh asked.

"Biggies don't get into this story."

"They should," said Josh. "The Bible says human beings are the highest creation."

"Not to chickens, they ain't. Look, buddy. You gonna keep your beak shut?"

"Sorry," he said.

"Tarkah still lays her eggs. Her children needed light to fly and hunt and scratch for worms. So every day Tarkah lays an egg of fire and sends it spinning across the sky. The fire

goes out. Earth egg sleeps. Next morning Tarkah lays a new fire egg. That's the story, buddy, and that's why chickens lay eggs in the morning and sing egg songs. It's how they say thanks to Tarkah."

Josh nudged her. "Now tell me the Tarkah story about snow. You know, Tarkah's feathers."

The old hen settled closer to his chest. "Another day. I'm tired."

"You won't forget to show me the fox hole in the morning?"

"Yeah, yeah, yeah."

"I got you the brew, Semolina."

"I told you, buddy, a deal is a deal."

"Okay." Holding her against his shirt, he stood up and walked back to the house. "You can sleep on my bed, but if Grandma comes while I'm in the bathroom, you'd better skedaddle out to the porch mighty quick. She says if she finds you in the house, something terrible is going to happen. You hear me?"

Semolina didn't answer. She was tucked in the crook of his arm, her head under her wing, and she was already asleep.

• • •

Tarkah's new fire egg rose behind the Binochette cows and cast long morning shadows over the grass. On the other side of the fence, Josh turned on the sprinklers over the Miller acres of Swiss chard. Watering was done early before the fierce heat—otherwise the fire egg would suck up the moisture from the leaves and shrivel them like old paper. Josh wiped his hands on his jeans. In the cool air, the sprinklers made a mist that changed to rainbows where the sun caught it. "Can chickens see rainbows?" he asked Semolina, who was following at a distance.

"Sure! But rainbows ain't nothing to crow about," clacked Semolina, who didn't like rain from clouds or sprinklers. "Chicken with her head in the air misses the worms."

Josh smiled. "When my baby sister is born, I'm going to bring her out here and show her the very first rainbow of her life."

"Might be a rooster."

"A boy? Nope. Mom says it's a girl, and I guess she knows. You hatch out many chickens, Semolina?"

She stretched one leg, then the other. "Ain't it time to go back?"

Josh would not be put off. "Family, Semolina. Did you ever have any little chickies?"

"Sure, buddy." She shook her feathers in a sassy way. "I adopted you, didn't I?"

"Me?" He laughed. "Wait a minute. You don't have me. I have you. You're supposed to be my pet."

"Who says, buddy?"

"I do."

"I say different." She pecked his shoe tie, pulled it undone and let it drop. "You going to stand here crowing all day? Or you wanna see the fox hole?"

The hens in number three were still roosting and half asleep when Josh opened the barn. As he and Semolina walked in, there was a stirring of feathers that sounded like a wind, then a shifting of feet and a movement of hundreds of red combs as heads turned, eyes snapping alert. Semolina led Josh the full length of the barn and came to a standstill by the end wall.

The rustling behind them stopped. There was such a stillness that Josh imagined every hen to be holding its breath.

He looked up and down the black boards. He and Tucker had gone over every inch of these walls, and he knew them as well as he knew his own bedroom. "No hole here," he said.

For answer, Semolina scratched away some of the ground straw, then pushed her beak against the side of a tarred slat. The length of lumber swung aside, revealing a triangle of darkness about ten inches wide at the bottom and peaking some fifteen inches up.

Josh sucked in breath and let it out in a low whistle. "So

that's the hole!" He put his hand through and touched something familiar, a piece of eggshell. "The board's got only one nail in it. It swings. Wow! The chickens push it aside and deliberately lay their eggs out there—for the fox." He dropped right down on his stomach to see through the hole. It was like a little cave out there, dark and airless. "This must be behind the straw pile!" he said. "Spittin' bugs! No wonder we didn't see anything from the outside."

He got up on his hands and knees and looked around the shed. The chickens were so still they could have all been solid blocks of ice. "They're scared, aren't they?" he said to Semolina. "Scared what the fox will do."

She didn't answer. Nor would she in front of all her kin. Silently, she led him out of the barn. As soon as he closed the door behind them, the chickens started the biggest racket he'd ever heard. Not egg songs. Not cries for food. It was a yackety-yack noise that reminded him of a bus full of kids on the first day of school.

Semolina walked fast, her claws scrabbling in the dust. He followed her along the length of laying boxes to the back of the barn, where the straw was piled high. Sure enough,

there was a tunnel behind the straw, widening against the wall to nest size. Here the dried grass was smooth, packed down and showing bits of old shell where the fox had eaten his fill of eggs before carrying more away to his lair.

"You betcha they're scared," said Semolina. "Chickens got reason to be scared of most things—hawks, foxes, biggies." She turned her head. "Most of all biggies."

Josh was too excited to argue with her. He picked her up in both hands and kissed her right on top of her wicked old head. She blinked, pulled away, and he put her down again. "My dad is going to be a happy man," he said.

"Yeah?"

"Very happy."

"Happy like in giving the chicken a big reward?"

"Reward?" Josh laughed. "That's another new word! Semolina, where do you learn all this stuff?"

She stretched one wing, then the other, and said in a sniffy voice, "Buddy, I ain't no dumb cluck. Tell him I want more brown water."

• • •

Tucker nailed that loose board so tight that an elephant couldn't have pushed it aside. Then to make doubly sure, he nailed another plank across the outside of the barn.

"Son, you were right on target about that fox. I feel mighty ashamed pushing words back down your mouth like that. Pete Binochette just told me. He said it hangs out in the woods, big red fellow, slippery as custard. Beats me how you knew."

Josh handed him another nail. "You know how I knew. Semolina."

Tucker smiled and shook his head. "I'm reminded of my aunt Maureen, who lived in Columbus, Ohio. Well, she was a fine woman, mighty fond of talk. When she told us something she'd heard in town, she'd add, 'And if it's not true, it's a good story.'"

Josh folded his hands across his stomach and stared at the nailed-up wall. Tucker had given him this lecture before.

"When I was young, I set that in my mind. Truth is truth, and a good story is a good story. We get them mixed up and we're in trouble, Josh. I seen fine people mess up their brains not knowing which is which."

Josh felt his eyes prick with tears. He lowered his head and said in a slow, easy way, "If Semolina doesn't talk to me, how come I knew about the hole?"

His father got his sad, soft look. "Don't get me wrong, son. I know that old chicken's smart—more cunning than a jungle of monkeys. I believe she could lead you to the hole. But talking human talk?"

"She does." Josh swallowed. His throat was getting thick.

Tucker got to his feet and stepped away from the wall. Putting his long hand on Josh's shoulder, he bent over until their faces were level. "Josh, sometime you go stand by the mirror and watch the ways your lips move with words. Folks' mouths are made for folks' language. It's the gift God gave us. In the beginning was the word. When you done that, you look again at the shape of a chicken's beak. Bird talk. That's all it's made for. Come on, let's have ourselves some lunch." And Tucker was striding away toward the house before Josh had a chance to say, but Dad, what about parrots?

• • •

In the yard, the first thing Josh saw was his patchwork quilt, wet on the clothesline. He guessed why, but Grandma told him anyway. "Chicken poop!" she said. "That filthy bird in your room! On your bed! Haven't I told you a dozen times? I didn't come five hours on a train to clean a menagerie. I declare, that scrawny chicken gets in your room one more time and I pack my bags."

Josh crawled under the house where Semolina was leaning against the base of the chimney. "You okay?"

"Yeah, yeah." Semolina looked weary. "I got chased with a broom."

"You had an accident on my bed."

"It happens," she said. "It happens."

"It happens with brown water," Josh told her.

"Where's the thanks?" she snapped. "Where's good Semolina! Well done, Semolina! You saved the eggs from the fox, Semolina!"

"I'm sorry." He reached out to stroke some cobwebs off her feathers, but she backed away.

"Never trust a biggie," she said.

"You can trust me, you silly old bird." He smiled. "I'm your pet, remember? Your little chickie?" He tucked his hands under his arms and wagged his elbows. "Cluck, cluck, cluck!"

She ignored him.

"You adopted me!" he insisted.

She lifted the foot with the silver ring and came one step closer. "What's for lunch?"

"I don't know, but I'll find out. You want room service?"

She gave him a sharp-eyed look. "Under-room service, and don't forget the ketchup."

That evening, Grandma said she was too tired to go to the hospital, and Josh was more pleased than he thought he should have been. He and Tucker would have Elizabeth to themselves, just the three of them as always. He picked some yellow flowers from the garden and imagined his mother's face when he told her about that rotten old fox and the hole in the shed. She'd be so pleased. Not that she worried about things like foxes and missing eggs, but she sure worried about Tucker being worried.

The long hospital corridor, smelling of antiseptic and dry linen, was lit with the last light of day. Another of Tarkah's eggs about to disappear, thought Josh as he strode out ahead of his father. Lights were switched on in some of the rooms, but Elizabeth's room was almost dark. Josh stopped with a feeling of dread. His mother was lying on her pillow, eyes closed, the tube in her arm.

Tucker wasn't prepared for this either. He went to the bed and put his hand on his wife's forehead. She opened her eyes and smiled at him. Josh heard her say, "Bleeding again."

Bleeding? What did that mean? He pushed in beside his father and looked down at the needle in the back of her hand. It was the same as the day she came in here, a tube that went all the way up the bed to a bag of fluid on a metal stand. His throat went dry. "What's gone wrong?"

Her free hand went to the back of his head and pulled him down so that she could kiss him. "Nothing's wrong. This is a way to take medicine that's too bad to swallow."

He knew she was pretending. "Is it the baby?" he asked.

Elizabeth glanced at Tucker, then she smoothed Josh's

hair away from his forehead. "Honey, the baby's okay. We had a little scare this afternoon, but now everything's fine."

"You sure?" He put his head down on the pillow against hers. Her hair was as thick as Annalee's, but it smelled of hospital. "I wish you'd come home, Mom. We'd look after you real good."

"I wish too, but this is the best place for me right now. Josh, if I were a chicken, no farmer would ever want me. I'm such a bad layer. Chickens have the sense to hold on to their eggs until they're ready to be laid. My body doesn't want to wait. You know what happens to a baby if it's born too soon?"

He nodded.

"This is one busy little baby. I think she's going to be a ballet dancer. But she's small. We have to give her as much time as we can, and that's the reason for the medication." She eased herself up in the bed and took a deep breath. "All right, my two guys. How are things back at the ranch?"

She was interested in all of it, the hole in the shed, Semolina, the quilt, Grandma, the big red fox, but her smile disappeared

when Tucker said that Pete Binochette and his farmhands had a hunting party in the woods. "No!" she said. "Why kill it? The fox is just being a fox."

"Mom, he's been stealing our eggs!" said Josh.

"They're the chickens' eggs," she reminded him. "We steal them too, only we think we have that right. So does Mr. Fox. Tucker, darling, can't they set a snare trap and catch it alive?"

"What then?" said Tucker.

"There must be wilderness sanctuaries for foxes. It's not a good thing to take a life if you don't have to. Talk to Pete! Please! Don't let him shoot it."

Tucker nodded and scratched the back of his neck. "Well, yeah, I guess."

She folded her hands on her round stomach and turned to Josh. "Tell me about your boat," she said.

Chapter Six

THE DAYS WENT BY AS SLOW AS molasses in January, and still that big red fox wasn't caught. Farmers talked of sightings. Two of the ducks from the Binochettes' pond disappeared, and Mrs. Waters lost a loaf of bread she'd left to cool on a window ledge, although that might have been a hungry dog. Still, the fox managed to dodge every trap and snare and hunting party. Tucker wasn't worried. He'd hammered

the board across the hole with four-inch nails. His egg count was way up again and all his chicken houses were as safe as Fort Knox.

It was Semolina who was fretting. Rumors were running through the chicken barns, and none of them gave the old hen much comfort. "Fox knows I spilled the beans," she said. "I'm on his hit list."

"Don't worry," Josh tried to soothe her. "They'll catch that fox anytime now and ship him clear out of town."

"They'll never catch him!" Semolina shivered. "Tell your father to shoot him deady bones. They got to do that. Or else . . . !" She closed her eyes.

"I'll look after you," he said.

Most days, Semolina walked at Josh's heels, jumpy as a cricket, and at night she insisted that he lock her inside the tractor shed—which was safe enough, having a concrete floor and steel walls. He let her out each morning when he watered the Swiss chard.

Josh begged Grandma to allow Semolina back in his bedroom, but she wasn't having any of that. "Filthy old bird! I told you before, if she comes in, I move out."

"What if the fox gets her?"

Grandma smiled, showing all her teeth. "Bring her to me and I'll give her to the fox! Here, Mr. Fox! Nice little snack, Mr. Fox!"

Josh swallowed back bitter hatred. Forgive people, always forgive people. He chanted his mother's words as he walked away, clenching and unclenching his fists. Forgive us our trespasses as we forgive those who trespass against us. Saying it didn't make a speck of difference. Grandma might be his mother's mother, but she was downright miserable, cantankerous mean.

After that, Josh stayed away from the house as much as

possible. When he wasn't helping Tucker in the barns or Annalee with egg sorting, he worked on his boat in the tractor shed, sanding down the hull to get it ready for painting. Now it looked like a real boat, two seats fore and aft, a metal plate on the stern to hold the outboard and fittings for the oarlocks. There were only three coats of paint between Josh and the river. He'd take Annalee out fishing before the end of the summer vacation.

Semolina, nervous of the tractor shed's open door, roosted among old tools in the rafters above Josh's head.

He told her he'd heard the fox was over on the other side of town. "The guys at Semco told Dad—big red fox down at Loon Lake."

"Semco," repeated Semolina.

"The place we go every week." Josh sometimes forgot that Semolina couldn't read. "Sampson Egg Marketing Company," he added, hoping she wouldn't take offense.

But Semolina was too jittery about the fox to get political. "Don't matter where the fox is. He's got his gang on the lookout. Ferrets and wildcats, raccoons and rats. Word from the girls is, they got this place staked out."

"Semolina, you been watching too much television."

"I don't get to watch nothing excepting my back," she snapped.

Josh blew ahead of the sandpaper, and a fine wood dust filled the air. "Why would a fox have a gang? Semolina, that doesn't make an inch of sense. Foxes always work alone."

"Carriers," she said.

"Carriers?"

She put her beak in the air. "Excuse me. I didn't tell you foxes don't have shopping carts. Most eggs a fox carries is two or three in his mouth. Takes him all night to shift a hundred eggs. So he has a carrier gang. Raccoons, rats, pack of thieving critters. Now nobody ain't getting no eggs, and they're all after the one that got the hole closed."

"You're safe here in the tractor shed." Josh ran his hand over the hull, now smooth enough for the first primer coat. "When Grandma goes, you'll come back in the house."

"I might be deady bones by then," she said gloomily.

"Don't think like that. It isn't healthy." He looked at her. "Semolina, you never told me if you had a family."

She shifted on her perch. "No, I never."

"Never told me? Or never had chicks?"

"Both," she said.

"You could still have babies. You ever thought about that?"

She made a coughing noise. "Excuse me, buddy. You might know biggies, but you don't know birds. I ain't laid an egg in four years, and even then . . . " She stopped and put her head on one side. "How do I say this? One bird don't make life. It needs two."

"No rooster?"

"You got it. No rooster."

"Spittin' bugs, Semolina, I knew that all along. But if you had a hankering for a family, we could get you some fertile eggs. You still go broody?"

"Don't get personal!"

"Sorry. I just wanted you to know— if you get that brood itch to sit on eggs, you tell me. I'd get eggs for you. Mr. Pojurski, he's got hens and roosters."

A membrane came over her eye. "I might be fox supper by then."

Josh wished she'd shut up about the fox. He knew if he hadn't insisted she show him the hole in the number-three barn, she wouldn't be in this sad, shivery state, scared stiff about being slowly chewed by an angry fox. "Tell me another Tarkah story," he said.

She was silent.

"The one about snow. Go on."

"I told it last winter."

"Tell me again."

Semolina opened her beak. "I ain't in the mood, but here goes, buddy. Tarkah laid a fire egg every day so her chick-

ens on the big earth egg could have heat and light. All the chickens were busy, busy, busy. Every day was new life, and the birds were tired. Tarkah said, 'My children need a rest time.' So she plucked out her breast feathers, white and soft, and dropped them down on the earth egg. The earth egg turned white and too cold for new life. That's why animals and birds do not make young in the time of Tarkah's feathers. You know all this, buddy. I told you before. Winter is slow time. But some animals like the fox, they don't rest." She shivered. "Sun egg or moon egg, fast time or slow time, foxes hunt chickens with big sharp teeth."

Josh locked Semolina in the tractor shed the day he went to town with Tucker and Annalee. It was Semolina's idea. She'd talked herself into such a terror that she insisted on having the door bolted while Josh was away.

"You don't have to worry," he told her. "If I'm not here, I'll lock you in, just like I lock you in at night, end of story."

It was a mighty big building for one scrawny little chicken.

The tractor, plow and harrows were at one end with Tucker's old motorcycle and several drums of oil and diesel. At the other end were Josh's boat and a thick wooden workbench that ran the length of the wall. Across the rafters, Tucker had nailed sheets of chipboard to hold storage boxes, old garden tools and spare hoses for the sprinkler system. Semolina fluttered from the oil drum to the workbench and up into the rafters, where no fox was likely to find her.

Josh said she could roost where she liked as long as she promised to stay off his boat. "You know you're a lot safer here than under the house," he told her.

Tucker had promised that on this egg trip, they could pick up the outboard and get marine paint at the boat store. If that wasn't good news enough, Annalee had asked if she could come along too for the ride.

Josh scrubbed up extra smart, put on his nearly new jeans and combed his hair with Brylcreem. Annalee was so pretty that sitting next to her made his breath hurt in his chest. She had on a dress with a skirt that spread over the backseat

of the car and touched his knee. Her lipstick was pink and so shiny it made her mouth look wet. He stared at her and forgot to talk.

Tucker drove carefully, the egg trailer swinging along behind them. No missing eggs these days. The trailer had *Sampson Egg Marketing Company* painted across each side. It was filled with wooden pallets that were in turn stacked with cartons of eggs sorted by Annalee and Josh. They would leave the full Semco trailer at the Sampsons' warehouse and take an empty one back to the farm.

Sampsons' was a mile or so out the other side of town, but Tucker pulled up in the main street. He turned to the backseat with his big slow smile. "You kids hop out here and amuse yourselves. When I'm done with Sampsons', I expect I'll find you near the marine shop."

Josh scrambled out and held the door open for Annalee. He'd been to town with her before heaps of times, but not this year, not with her so growed up and looking like a movie star. When his father drove away, there was just the two of them on the sidewalk in the hot sun. Josh knew he should say something, but his mouth was dry and there weren't any

words. It was a relief when Annalee clapped and said, "Let's go to Duigan's ice cream parlor. My treat."

They crossed the sunbaked street and pushed through glass doors to cool shade and the familiar smells of fudge, lime and caramel. Most of the tables and booths were full, and the staff was running around, busy as fleas at a dog show. Duigan's hired high school kids during the vacation. Some of them started not knowing how to make a sundae or do a real thick shake, but they soon learned.

When Annalee walked up to the counter, the guys stared and someone whistled. Josh moved closer to her. She put her hand on his shoulder and said, "What are you having, Josh?"

He stood taller. "Butter pecan, waffle cone."

"One scoop or two?"

"One. What are you having?"

"Same." She leaned against the counter and called out her order to one of the kids, who was still staring at her. He was tall and skinny with silver-edged glasses and a rim of black fluff like chicken feathers on his top lip. He gave her the biggest grin. "You didn't tell me you were coming in today."

Annalee smiled. "Bob, meet my neighbor Josh Miller. Remember I told you about the boat he's building?"

Josh stopped breathing. Bob! Was this toe ring Bob?

"Hi, Josh." Bob leaned over the counter, holding out his hand. "Annalee's told me heaps of stuff about you. She reckons you're like a little brother."

Josh stepped back and shoved his hands in his pockets. "She's already got a little brother," he said.

Bob quickly became another of Josh's worry wrinkles. It felt bug-spittin' bad hating someone who was so nice. Bob said he and Annalee were going to the movies Saturday and would Josh like to come too? Josh said no, he was going to see his mother. Bob said he forgot that she was in the hospital, and he hoped she was okay. Seven months pregnant, said Annalee. Near eight months, said Josh, and Mom was okay, they were all okay, everything top of the pops okay. Bob said how about if he came out to see the boat sometime? Josh said, what time? It was busy on the farm. Sorry. Besides, no point seeing the skiff before it was finished. Sorry, sorry. Then Bob made him a butter pecan sundae with hot fudge, whipped cream and cherries—on the house, he said.

They came to visit anyway, on egg-sorting day, Harrison and Bob led up to the tractor shed by Annalee, who was telling them how Josh was going to take her fishing on the river. He had to show them the boat. Well, truth was, he actually liked showing them the boat. The paint was only at undercoat stage, but it looked real good, white, smooth, classic, he had to admit.

Harrison forgot to be a smart-aleck. He ran his hands over the bow. "Neat, Slosh! I didn't know a kid could make a real boat like this. Would you show me how you did it?"

Josh unrolled the plans on the tractor bench, and they all bent over them while he talked them through the long process stage by stage—laminating the beech wood, cutting out the stern and the stays, solid bronze screws and glue for the joints, strips of ply bent over the steaming boiler, more gluing, caulking, sanding, painting, fitting the stern plate for the motor, the oarlocks. They were impressed.

"You've done a fine professional job," Bob said.

"What do you mean fine?" said Annalee. "It's hog-snorting brilliant!"

Bob said he wanted to build a small sailboat to take out on Loon Lake, and he thought now maybe he could if he got the right plans.

Harrison couldn't keep his hands off the skiff. "Can I come fishing too?" he begged.

Right-way up and gleaming white, Josh could clearly see it was a boat to be admired. Longer and wider than his bed, it had a shallow curve to the hull and a nicely flared bow, the

sort of boat that would be stable on the river. There were two bench seats in it, one in the bow behind the oarlocks, the other nearer the stern. Under the seats was space for two polystyrene flotation blocks that would make the skiff unsinkable. The Johnson five-horse power motor was standing proud against the wall next to two brand-new varnished eight-foot oars.

Grandma didn't usually come to the tractor shed, but a visit from the Binochette children brought her out with a jug of lemonade and some applesauce muffins. "So this is the famous boat," she said, looking it over. "Well, each to his own fancy, I always say." She poured lemonade for Annalee. "Joshua is crazy about boats. Always has been. Funny obsession for a dryland chicken boy." She brought the jug to Josh. "I will say this for my grandson. When he does something, he makes a good job of it. Doesn't get that from either of his parents."

She walked away, leaving a silence in the shed. Josh picked

up a muffin and wrapped it in a paper napkin. "I'll save this one for Semolina."

Bob looked blank for a second, then he hit his forehead with the palm of his hand. "Your pet chicken!" he said. "The chicken wearing the ring I won at the fair!"

"Yeah." Josh smiled. Annalee forgot to tell him the ring had come from a fair. So they hadn't bought it special from a jewelry store, like some kind of going-steady ring.

"I have to see this crazy bird," Bob said. "Annalee says it practically pecked the ring off her toe."

Josh's smile faded. He turned to Annalee. "Wasn't Semolina in the egg room with you?"

"No."

"Then she must still be here." He peered in the dark corners under the eaves. "Semolina? Semolina!"

There was no movement, no rustle of feathers.

"Semolina! Applesauce muffin!"

"Maybe she's under the house," Annalee said.

Josh shook his head. "No. She doesn't go there anymore. She's always here or in the egg room." He felt a tightening in his stomach. He went to the door of the shed and yelled for her.

The others came out. Side by side, they stood outside the door, calling for all they were worth, "Semolina! Semolina!"

Tucker came out of the number-one chicken house, a wrench in his hand. "What happened?"

Josh didn't know if anything had happened, but he was feeling bad. When had he last seen her? He wasn't sure. Lately he'd grown careless. He hadn't always closed the door.

"You kids all right?" Tucker yelled.

"Semolina's missing," Annalee replied.

Chapter Seven

FOR THE REST OF THE DAY, UNTIL dark, they hunted for Semolina. They called her name from one end of the farm to the other, walked the rows of Swiss chard, crawled under the house. Inside, they went through every room with Grandma not saying a word and searched all closets, bins, boxes lest she got shut in somewhere. Josh even checked the laundry cupboard.

They found nothing, not even a stray feather.

Josh's bad feeling got worse when they looked in the number-three chicken house. The hens in number three had been squawking as though they had a big conference going. When Josh opened the door, they flew up, filling the air with dust and feathers and noise. It might have been because the other kids were with him, but he thought not. Most times those chickens were so quiet a stranger could lift them out of the straw and stroke their feathers.

Come evening, there was such dread in him, he didn't want Bob and the Binochettes to go home. "I think it's the fox," he said.

"She could have hidden in the woods," said Annalee.

"Why would she go into the woods?"

"If the fox came looking, she could have run anywhere. She could even be on our farm." She put her arm around his shoulders. "Don't worry, Josh, we'll look for her tomorrow."

Josh wanted to hold on to hope, but the bad feeling wouldn't go away. Sure, it was possible that Semolina had gotten scared

and run for the woods or the Binochettes' farm—only if something was chasing her, she'd never make it, her being old and not much of a runner. You could be certain if a fox had her in his sights, she'd be sitting meat.

These thoughts so filled his head that he couldn't eat his supper. He mashed the tuna sauce and pasta with his fork and worry-wrinkled about trying not to blame Grandma. Tonight, though, tonight he was going to leave his window wide open, and if Semolina jumped through it, she could poop all over his quilt if she wanted. Then Grandma would pack her bag and go home and he and Semolina could be together and happy again.

Grandma had poured herself a big helping of brew. She stared at him across the froth on the glass. "Don't fret," she said. "She'll come home when she's hungry." Then she turned to Tucker. "Saw his boat today. Good job for a young one. It's in his blood. Elizabeth told you my granddaddy was a sea captain?"

Tucker put down his fork. "No! I don't think she knows that!"

Grandma sniffed. "Memory on her like a bottomless

bucket. Captain of a collier, he was, a coal ship—" She stopped and said briskly, "Josh, you need a tissue?"

He realized that tears were running down his nose and dropping onto his plate. He shook his head and leaned sideways to get a handkerchief out of his jeans pocket. What he pulled out was a paper napkin full of squashed applesauce muffin.

He didn't say anything while Tucker told Elizabeth. He was all right until his mother's eyes filled up with water and she said, "Oh, Josh! Dear, dear Semolina!" Then in one movement he was out of the hospital chair and onto the bed beside her, his head against her shoulder, crying wetness on her nightgown. She held him, her fingers tracing little circles on the back of his head. "Josh, I'm so sorry."

Tucker said, "Danged chicken could have run off into the woods."

Josh shook his head against his mother's hand.

"You must be feeling very sad," she said.

A voice in his head was yelling, It's Grandma's fault! Semolina's gone because of Grandma! He might have said it out loud except that Tucker spoke first. "Probably no fox," said Tucker. "She's old. Animals do that. They know when their time comes and off they go, just themselves, to lay down in some quiet place."

Again Josh shook his head.

Elizabeth massaged his scalp and the back of his neck, and her fingers felt as if they were a part of him. "I'll tell you a secret, Josh. Sad always comes with happy. That's true. Always. But sad is so big, we don't see the happy thing."

What was she talking about?

"So—do you want me to tell you the happy thing?"

He thought for a moment, then nodded.

"This little baby is putting on weight. She's a whole eight months grown and the doctor says she's out of danger."

He raised his head to look at her. "You're coming home?"

The silence was too long. He put his head down again, wiping his wet cheek on her pillow.

"Not until she's born." Elizabeth hugged him. "We're going to call her Tori. On paper it'll be Victoria, like you're Joshua. Josh and Tori Miller. Does that sound like a happy thing?"

She wanted him to nod, so he did.

Tucker cleared his throat. "I'm thinking it's too early to think sad. That crafty old bird might be on the back porch waiting for us to get home."

"Could be," said Elizabeth. "Could well be."

Then Josh felt it. His mother's round belly suddenly moved like it was trying to push him clean off the bed. He sat up, astonished. "The baby kicked me!" he said.

That night he opened his bedroom window as wide as it would go. When Grandma came in to say good night, she looked at the window but kept hush about it. As she was going out the door, she turned and shook her head at him. "Animals don't live as long as us, Josh. That's a hard, God-given fact."

. . .

The search resumed in the morning, Annalee and Harrison hollering for Semolina on their cow farm while Josh, sick to his stomach, looked for her in the woods. Everyone called it the woods, but it wasn't big, no more than five acres of county land between the chicken farm and a loop in the river. The trees were mostly young, oak and sycamore, beech and elder and a few mountain ash already red with berries. The undergrowth was soft and trodden down in paths that wandered without purpose.

"Semolina!"

A blue jay flew off a low branch.

"Semolina? You there?" His voice was thick and wobbly.

Here there was no answering echo. The green was like a thick sponge that soaked up even his footsteps. He bent over, looking on the ground for animal sign, fox or raccoon, but he didn't see a thing except some deer prints in the wet nearer the river.

"Semolina!" This time her name was almost a whisper.

The worst thing was not knowing. His mind wrapped itself around the emptiness, and he felt a great hurting heaviness in his chest. This was absolutely the worst worry wrinkle of his entire life.

When he arrived at the house, they were out front, Grandma with her knitting on the porch chair and Tucker standing on the step, one hand holding the pole. They'd been talking but stopped when they saw him.

He trailed his feet over the near bald lawn. "Nothing in the woods."

Grandma put down her knitting. "About your age, I had a cat called Smithy. My father backed the car over him."

The suddenness of her words shocked him. "Was he all right?"

"What do you think?"

He had to know. "Did he die? Grandma, was he killed?"

The sun glinted on her glasses, and he couldn't see what was going on in her eyes. "You'll get over it." She stood up,

one hand on the middle of her back, and went in the house, walking awkwardly as though her legs had gone to sleep.

Tucker let go of the pole and took a couple of slow steps toward him. He hooked his thumbs low down in his suspenders and breathed deep through his nose. After a while, he said, "You okay?"

"I just wish I knew where she was," Josh said.

"She's gone, son." Tucker bent down. "Sorry. It's bad news."

Josh stared at him.

Slowly, Tucker unhooked his thumbs and put both hands on Josh's shoulders. He looked hard into his son's face and then said, "You better come with me."

Tucker led Josh to the straw pile at the back of chicken barn three. Walking sideways, Tucker pushed through to the back of the pile, where the egg nest had been. He beckoned Josh to follow.

On the ground, below the nailed-up board, lay a puddle of dark blood mixed with reddish brown feathers. In the middle of it, bent out of shape, lay the silver ring.

Chapter Eight

TUCKER HELD A PLASTIC BAG open while Josh scooped up the feathers with a trowel. Some of the feathers were small and soft, breast feathers, like Tarkah's snow except they were brown. He got every one, picking bits of fluff off straw, put it all in the bag. His eyes and nose were running, but he paid no heed to that. He needed to get every part of

her, blood too, even if it meant digging up the ground under the little blood spots that led away from the puddle.

Tucker didn't mention blood. He didn't need to. Chickens had white flesh and their blood came from deep inside.

"I think it was quick," was all Tucker said.

Josh said nothing. It had happened. Semolina had been eaten by the fox.

He carried the plastic bag back to the house. The lawn, clothesline, porch all shivered and swam in his tears, but the terrible feeling in him had gone. Now there was no feeling at all. He walked like a robot up the steps and across to the porch swing. In silence, he held the bag out to show Grandma.

She did a very strange thing. She lifted the bottom of her apron and put it over her head.

Josh looked for a fitting funeral box, but there was nothing in the house except an empty cereal box that Grandma took from a kitchen cupboard. He didn't want to put Semolina's remains in something as ordinary as a breakfast food box, but

the pictures on the box had a rightness to them, sunshine on a farm, rows of corn, milk pouring onto a bowl of golden cornflakes. It made him think of all the times Semolina had sat by his bowl, dipping her beak into his breakfast.

As he took the box, Grandma said, "I hope you're not fretting over what I said about the fox."

He looked at her. "You mean about giving her to him?"

"That and some."

He shrugged.

"You are," she said. "I recognize a fret when I see one. I didn't mean a scrap by it, you know. I worry about things. Your mother will tell you. I give tongue."

He looked down at the cereal box, fair busting with happy pictures.

"Spit it out," she said.

"You said to Mom—" He wriggled his feet.

"What did I say?"

"You said something about thoughts making things happen. Did you—" He stopped.

"Did I wish the fox into eating your chicken?" She sat with a thump that skidded the chair. "God save us, boy!

Nothing of the kind! I just say things. I get tired. You know how little kids get when they're tired? Well, it happens when you're old too. I worry. I worry about mess. I worry about you and the baby. I worry about my daughter's lack of ambition. I worry about the grass not growing on that godforsaken lawn and I worry about blocked drains. You got it in you. You're a worrier too, and one day you'll know what I'm talking about."

He knew already, and he vowed sure as eggs, he'd never let his worries make him say mean things to people, no matter how old he got.

"It's okay, Grandma," he said. Then he added, "I'm sorry about your father running over your cat."

Annalee and Harrison came over for the funeral. Annalee gave him a card from Bob, a real sympathy card with silver flowers, a poem on the outside and a message on the inside in Bob's writing.

"It's nice considering he never met Semolina," she said. "I did tell him about her, how smart she was and all that."

Josh wondered what else she'd told him. *Gee, Bob, it's so funny. Josh thinks Semolina actually talks to him.*

Not that it mattered now.

Tucker dug a hole for Semolina in the flower garden outside the kitchen window. He said the ground wasn't as hard as the rest of the yard, and besides, its meant that durn old bird was close to her favorite feeding place. He'd taken some care with the hole. It was next to a flowering geranium bush, neatly square with dirt in a little pyramid beside it.

Josh took the plastic bag out of the cereal box so Annalee and Harrison could have a last look. The blood and dirt had mixed up with the feathers, but the silver ring was plain as day, a bit twisted but still shining. Josh wondered if Annalee wanted it back. She didn't. He carefully put the plastic bag back in the cereal box, and fitted it into the hole.

"Wait," said Annalee. "We need to say something."

"Like what?" said Harrison.

"Maybe a memory or something. I remember how Semolina used to crouch on my feet when I was sorting eggs. She was warm. Her feathers felt like old curtains. I remember

when she saw that toe ring, she pecked it. Jeepers, it hurt. She was so intent on having that ring."

Josh was silent. It was hard to think about Semolina as a memory.

"I know a poem," said Harrison. He stood straight and saluted. "Beg your pardon, Joshua Hardon, there's a chicken in your garden." He looked at Josh. "Sorry. *Miller* doesn't rhyme with *garden*."

For a moment they stood looking at the bright top of the cereal box. Josh didn't speak, so Annalee said, "Okay. At funerals they always have a prayer. Who wants to say it?"

"You," said Josh. "Please?"

Annalee breathed deeply like someone about to swim underwater. "Dear God. Half of Semolina is here and the other half is in a fox. Let this geranium bush always have the most beautiful flowers and let the fox—let it be smart and—and funny like Semolina, and—and—"

"And never eat chickens again," said Josh. "Amen."

As they scooped the dirt into the hole, Josh imagined the prayer floating upward like a soft white feather. He thought of the Tarkah stories and vowed that never again would he tell anyone that Semolina had talked to him. Her hard cackly voice would be his biggest memory, and he wouldn't share it with anyone. As he patted the dirt down, he said to Annalee, "Do you suppose that chickens think God is a big chicken?"

That night, Josh was sick to his stomach. Grandma said he looked pale and maybe it was the day that had done it. Tucker agreed but wondered if Josh was coming down with something. "It could be a virus," he said. "Just to be on the safe side, no hospital visit tonight."

Josh nodded. He didn't feel like going out. His head was

hot, the rest of him cold, and he was so tired that there was no energy in him for sadness. For a while he sat out by the new grave, hoping to feel something. The geranium bush was in deep shadow and the dirt under it looked as it usually did when the garden had been weeded. Tomorrow he would put a stone or a cross on it so his father wouldn't forget and dig her up. Yes, a memory stone with her name on it would be good. He went back inside and turned on the television.

Tucker came in, showered and wearing one of his best shirts. "Next month there's another batch of young chickens coming in. Fourteen weeks old. You want to choose one of them for a pet?"

Josh shook his head.

"Think about it," Tucker said.

Television was like a landscape rolling past a car window, of no interest to him. He got up, said good night to Grandma, who was sitting in Tucker's chair, knitting something small and pink. For a while he stood inside the door, looking at the orange light of sunset, another of Tarkah's eggs falling out of the sky. It was then he realized he had nothing of Semolina in his bedroom. This morning he had been careful to collect

all her remains, every little feather, yet he had not kept one feather back for himself. Everything was buried. It was as though she had never been.

He kicked off his shoes and lay on top of the bed, his hands behind his head, and although he was very tired, he did not sleep. He heard the car come back, heard Tucker coming to his room. "You awake, son?"

"Yeah."

Tucker put on the light and sat on the end of the bed. He had a sheet of white cardboard stuck with photographs of Josh and Semolina and messages from Elizabeth. On top of the card, his mother had written, *The Story of the Little Red Hen.*

"She made it for you," Tucker said.

Josh's eyes prickled as though they had sand in them, but he was too worn out for tears. His father must have searched for these photos and taken them up to the hospital. They'd done this together, Mom and Dad. There was a picture of him seven years old and laughing, Semolina dragging the meat out of his burger. In another, a picture he hadn't seen before, he was asleep, arms flung out, Semolina perched on his chest, her head under her wing. Eight—no, nine photos of Semolina.

These were better than feathers!

"Thanks, Dad," he said. "I'll put it on the wall."

Tucker nodded and scrubbed Josh's hair with his hand. "You okay, son? Maybe it's time to brush your teeth and get into your pajamas. Your grandma's a mite worried about you."

Josh swung his legs off the bed. "Grandma's always worried."

Tucker smiled, eyes half shut. "You only just found that out?"

Although the room was breathless warm, Josh dreamed of snow. Little white feathers were falling from the sky and piling up in the yard, soft as fluff but icy to the touch. They blew across the lawn, lay on the clothesline and covered the red geranium flowers with white. Josh needed to make a tombstone for Semolina in the shape of a big chicken. He knew exactly what to do. He gathered mounds of feathers, shaped and patted, and the white chicken seemed to grow by itself, beautiful, wings outstretched like an angel. Then something happened. The falling feathers were no longer snow

but hail. Little white stones rattled on the path and the tombstone chicken slid away in an avalanche of tiny ice pebbles. He couldn't save it from flattening out over the garden.

He woke, heart beating fast.

Outside, the sky was dark as pitch and brilliant with stars. He rolled over, his back to the window, and closed his eyes. Then it came again, the hail noise. Pebbles. No. Not pebbles! Something else!

He rolled to his knees on the bed and pushed up the window.

"You there, buddy?" rasped a familiar voice.

Chapter Nine

SEMOLINA LOOKED TERRIBLE. Half her feathers had gone, her eyes were shut and she was shivering sick.

"I thought you were dead!" he cried.

"Lift me up, buddy. I can't fly."

Josh was out that window like an arrow, scooping her up and holding her against his chest. "Semolina! Oh, wow! It's really you!"

She kicked against him and squawked with pain. "Fox!"

Instantly his touch became gentle. He reached through the window, placed her on the foot of the bed and then climbed back into the room. "What happened? We found your feathers. We had a funeral."

She was shivering. "Fox got me outside egg shed. I thought I was a goner. Rooty-tooty big fight. I shoved my beak in his front foot. He let go. I hid in straw. Stayed till morning. Then under the boat."

Josh put on his bedside light and looked at her. There were teeth marks on her bare, mottled back and a cut on her wing but no serious damage that he could see. He snatched his T-shirt from the floor and wrapped her in it. "We thought you had to be dead. There was so much blood."

Her eyes opened. "Told you, buddy. I got his paw."

A smile broke open inside Josh. He wanted to hold her and dance around the room. He sprawled across the bed, his face close. "We scooped up that blood, every drop. We buried it with your feathers."

"Excuse me! You buried my feathers with fox blood?" She struggled and freed herself from his shirt. "Me and fox?"

Then she thrust her beak against his nose. "Whatcha done with my ring?" she squawked.

He laughed. "Oh, Semolina, I love you! I love you so much!"

Josh thought of waking his father that instant, but the idea simmered down. Morning would do. Semolina was hurting and thirsty. He went into the bathroom to get her water in his mug, and as he turned off the tap, he had the sudden thought that her return might be just a dream. He spilled water on the floor running back to his room.

It was no dream. She was real and there, crouched under his T-shirt, her eyes half closed.

Twice during the night, he offered to look in the fridge. She wasn't hungry, she said, which told him surely she was in pain. The most comfortable place for her was on his chest, and that suited him real fine. He could feel her heart ticking against his and the rhythm of her breathing, the warmth of her on his skin, the occasional pricking of her claws. The old dusty Semolina smell was right there under his nose.

Something in him felt downright foolish for all the grief he'd spent thinking she was dead, but that didn't matter. This was the happy thing his mother talked about, only Mom had been wrong about the size of it. The happy thing was much, much bigger than the sad.

Semolina slept some of the time and so did he. When they were both awake, she told him what had happened. The fox had come after her in broad daylight and taken her by surprise. The girl biggie was sorting eggs in the shed and Semolina was pecking at the door to get in. Sudden smell of

fox! Too late! Fox grabbed her from behind and carried her, head hanging down, to the back of chicken house three. She knew what was coming. Revenge. Old fox was going to eat her by the nailed-up door. She struggled. Lost feathers. No good. He held her. So she gave it to him. Rooty-tooty fight. Beak into his front foot. Yelped, he did. Let go. Backed off, bleeding. She pushed into the straw, dug deep in where he couldn't reach her. He tried scratching with one paw. Then he gave up.

Josh sniffed her warm smell. "We were calling you. All over, we called you. For hours."

"Ain't no sound plum in the middle of a straw heap," she said.

First light, she nosed out of the straw. Fox had gone, but she was terrified he'd come back. She made it up to the tractor shed, found the door open. She'd lost wing feathers. Couldn't fly up to her usual roosting place. The only safe place was under the upturned skiff.

"Wasn't fox size. Squeezed the breath out of me. I figured you'd be along after breakfast."

"I didn't work on the boat yesterday."

"Yeah, yeah. So I noticed."

"I was hunting for you in the woods! Then we found your feathers. Annalee and Harrison came over and we had a funeral for you. I didn't go near the tractor shed all day."

She shifted and her claws pricked his skin. "Undo it," she said.

"What?"

"The funeral. Undo it. I want my ring."

First red light from the new Tarkah egg and Josh was out of bed. Semolina settled into the warm place he'd left, but not for long. Josh couldn't wait to share the happy thing with his father. "I'll carry you up the stairs. I won't hurt you."

"No!" Semolina snapped her eye at him. "Not the biggie with the broom!"

"Just Dad. Please?"

"Okay. But not the other one!"

At that moment, Josh had a thought that came at him like a bolt of lightning. Grandma and Semolina didn't get on because they were alike.

He put a folded bath towel over his hands like a cushion and carried the chicken up the stairs on it, careful so that his footsteps wouldn't jolt her. The door to his parents' room was closed, and with his hands full, he couldn't open it. He called several times. "Dad? Dad? Da-ad!"

Tucker gave an answering grunt.

"Open the door," Josh said. "I got a surprise for you."

Most times Tucker's emotions were middle range, neither hot nor cold, but when he saw Semolina, he got lit up like a firecracker, crying, "Well, bless my soul! It's a doggone miracle! That's what it is. Miracle!"

"Caw-awk!" clucked Semolina.

"It was fox's blood, Dad," said Josh. "She stuck her beak in his paw and he let her go. That's how she got away."

Tucker pulled back the curtains and beckoned them over to the window. In the early morning light, he looked at every part of the old chicken, lifting her wings, lightly touching the tooth marks. Then he looked at Josh, his eyes heavy with thought. "Ain't no fox, son."

"It was!" Josh insisted. "That same old red fox as stole the eggs."

Tucker rubbed his mouth. "That's an interesting theory, Josh."

"It's true!"

The sad, soft look came back, and Josh realized his dad was trying to find the best way of dealing with the old problem of the talking chicken. Tucker put his hand on Josh's head, the way the preacher man sometimes did after church. "We don't know that, son."

Josh didn't say anything. He'd made a promise to himself, he'd never again mention Semolina's talk, and he would keep that promise, no matter what.

"You see," said Tucker, "no chicken could fight off a fox. These bites are from a smaller animal, a ferret maybe. Years ago I seen a duck fight off a ferret. Looks like a ferret came snooping and they had a right old tussle. The bites ain't deep, but they're likely infected. We need to get her to the vet."

Josh nodded. His dad was right about that, at least. The chicken's pimply skin was red around the tooth holes.

There was a knocking at the door, and Grandma called out, "You wanting breakfast early, Tucker?"

"Come in, Augusta," said Tucker, and Semolina fluttered in alarm. She scrabbled over the towel, claws catching in the cotton, and tried to climb up Josh's shirt. Josh brought the towel up to cover her, but too late—Grandma was already in the room in her purple robe and slippers.

"Beg pardon," she said. "I thought you were all up. I heard you—oh my Lord! Is that the chicken?"

"She's alive," said Tucker. "It's a miracle!"

"Looks fifty percent dead," said Grandma, who wasn't wearing her glasses. "God help us! The fox has plucked her for the oven!"

"We think it was a ferret—or a rat," said Tucker.

Grandma poked Semolina. "She's cold. She's got the shakes."

Josh thought the spasms were from fear of Grandma, but he didn't like to say so. Grandma went back to her room and came out with some knitting, the little green coat she'd showed his mom at the hospital. She thrust the baby garment at Josh. "Here! Put this on her."

• • •

The black telephone in the kitchen grew warm with breath, Tucker calling the hospital to talk to Elizabeth, Josh waking up Annalee, Tucker asking the vet woman if he could have the first appointment at her clinic for his son's chicken bitten by a ferret.

Semolina wouldn't eat anything. She was awful tired and mostly wanted to rest. Josh felt he had to put the green knitting on her for Grandma's sake, but spittin' bugs, a baby's coat wasn't the most suitable cover for a chicken. Wings weren't arms. He draped it over her like a cape, did up the

top two buttons and let the sleeves hang. It looked stupid on her, but it was of some use. She stopped shivering, and when he next looked at her, she had her head under one of the sleeves and was asleep.

Tucker thought that the picnic basket was best for the trip to the vet. It was round with a double lid, and being of woven cane, the air got through. Although Grandma said nothing, she looked as though her tongue hurt from biting on it. "I'll scrub it after," Tucker told her, and she nodded. Of course, he'd never scrub it. Josh knew that. With Grandma, Tucker often made promises to keep peace.

Josh would have preferred to ride in the car with Semolina on his lap, but Tucker said she should be handled as little as possible to avoid spreading infection through her body. The towel was in the bottom of the basket, and she crouched on it asleep in the funny green jacket, every now and then twitching as if she was remembering the fox attack. Josh couldn't stop himself from lifting the lid to peek at her. "You can sit on the table anytime you like," he whispered.

The vet woman treated the old, half-plucked chicken as though it was the most beautiful bird on the planet. "All

right, Semolina, let's look at you. I love your coat. Do you mind if I unbutton it?" She pulled the overhead lamp down close to look at the red marks. "Mmm, it wasn't a ferret, that's certain."

Tucker shrugged. "I guessed some small critter—"

She shook her head. "A ferret would go for her throat. This animal had big jaws. I'd say a fox or maybe a dog."

Josh felt a ripple of surprise go through his father. Tucker gave him a quick look that Josh pretended not to notice.

"The damage looks worse than it is," said the vet. "There are no broken bones, no head trauma. She'll need antibiotics. I'll give you some powder to put in her food and a tube of ointment to apply three times a day. Good girl, Semolina. Do you want your coat back on?"

Tucker ran his hand over the back of his neck. "What's your guess? Dog? Or fox?"

"I'd bet on a fox." The vet did up the buttons on the green baby coat. "I don't know how she got away. Judging from the loss of feathers, I'd say she put up one heck of a fight." She patted Semolina with a finger light as a feather. "Brave girl!"

As they went back to the car, Josh sensed his father's unease. Tucker was troubled—not because he was wrong, but because he couldn't explain how Josh had been right. He looked hard at Josh as they opened the car, but all he said was, "Fox, eh?"

It was Josh's idea that they go by the hospital and take Semolina in to see Elizabeth. The suggestion didn't rest easy with Tucker. "It's real early. They might be busy. And a chicken?"

"The nurses won't mind. Dad, it's a picnic basket!"

Tucker relaxed into his slow smile. "So it is!" he said. "And if there was ever a day for a picnic, this is it!"

Elizabeth Miller was out of bed, arranging some flowers on the table by the window. She was surprised to see them, and she almost ran to hug them. Immediately she knew what was in the basket. "You've brought Semolina!"

"Are you supposed to be out of bed?" Tucker asked.

"Yes! Oh yes! Darling Tucker, I'm so well! We are both well, Tori and I. This is our best day yet." She lifted the lid

of the basket. "Semolina! Oh my goodness! The famous green coat, one hundred percent natural wool!" She put her hand to her mouth to hide laughter. "I can't think what Mother will say if she finds out!"

"Grandma gave it to her!" said Josh.

Elizabeth looked at Tucker, and he nodded. "Mother gave it to her?" she said. "That's a bigger miracle than Semolina escaping from the ferret!"

Tucker put his hands in his pockets. "The vet says—it was—probably a fox."

There was a short silence. Elizabeth said, "*The* fox?"

Tucker nodded again. "Likely."

She turned to Josh. "How did—"

But Josh had promised himself he wouldn't get into those old discussions again. He strolled over to the window and looked out at the clouds rolling in from the north. Thunderstorm by afternoon, he guessed. They needed good rain. River would swell and he'd be able to launch his boat.

Elizabeth sat in the chair. Her stomach was now so big it took up most of her lap, and the picnic basket was perched on the edge of her knees. She spoke to Semolina, and Semolina answered with a crooning cawk, cawk, letting Elizabeth know she was pleased to see her. Josh stood near, just in case the basket dropped, and he asked his mother, "Do you think chickens have a chicken god to look after them?"

"I wouldn't be at all surprised." She smiled. "People call God Father, so I guess chickens could call God Chicken and foxes could call God Fox. That seems logical."

"You mean there's a fox god too?"

"No. It the same god—one great creator Spirit, but we've

all got some of it in us, so we see it like ourselves. Does that make sense?"

"I—I think so."

"I guess it means we're all connected—chickens and foxes and rabbits and people." She took a deep breath, and her face looked shiny with happiness. "Oh, Josh, isn't this a wonderful world?"

"Sure is!" He reached out to hug her, the baby and the basket between them. The whole world was super-duper wonderful, and right now, he couldn't think of one single worry wrinkle.

Annalee came over after lunch, just as the weather was breaking. The thunder rolled around like marbles in a pan while big spots of rain hit the yard, disturbing dust. Semolina had eaten some bread soaked in milk and was now back in the picnic basket in Josh's room, with Grandma saying no more than "Not on the bed!"

Josh held the basket lid open while Annalee put antibiotic ointment on the bites. "You crazy bird! How did you get

away from that fox? This time yesterday we were so miserable! I never knew I could get that sad about a chicken. No! Don't peck me. This is ointment to make you better. Keep still! Don't you know I love you?"

The rain thickened, and soon a thin sheet of water lay on the rock-hard lawn. Josh looked out the window. "I have to dig up the box and get her silver ring."

"Don't bother," said Annalee. "We'll get another one."

Josh had to be careful with words. "I think she would like—I think I would like—to get the one we buried."

Annalee came out and held an umbrella over them both as he dug. The soft earth had turned to mud, so that the cereal box no longer looked cheerful. It was sodden and fell to bits as he pulled it out. He opened the plastic bag. This time, it wasn't chicken blood he smelled, but fox blood, and his nose wrinkled. He put in two fingers, pried out the strip of silver and closed the top as quick as he could.

"It's not a grave anymore," Annalee said.

She was right. There was no point in putting the feathers back in the hole. He troweled in muddy earth. Then they put the bag and the remains of the cereal box in the trash can.

. . .

That night he took some mashed potato and peas back to his room, mixed in Semolina's antibiotic powder and placed the bowl on the floor. She ate some and seemed a mite perkier. She was pleased to have her ring back. She held her leg out to look at it, then put her foot down and tested the ring with her beak to make sure it wouldn't come off. She wasn't up to much talking, though, and she still had the jitters. She was scared the fox would come after her again and didn't want the window open.

"I'll put the basket lids down," Josh said.

"Won't make no difference to that fox," she muttered.

"All right. Window open only one inch," he said. "That suit you?"

"Have it your way, buddy." She shrank down into the green coat and closed her eyes.

"You sound just like Grandma," he said as he turned toward the door.

Her indignant squawk stopped him. She had her head

over the edge of the basket, her yellow eye wide with anger. "What's that? What did you say?"

"It's okay, Semolina," he said. "It was only a joke."

But fact was, it wasn't.

He too went to sleep while the evening was still light. He hadn't realized he was exhausted until he put his head on the pillow and felt himself falling away into someplace deep, dark and gentle. When he woke, it was dark and Semolina wasn't in the basket. She was on the floor singing an egg song.

"Tarkah, tarkah, tark. Tarkah, tarkah, tark."

Josh sat up and put on the light. "What are you doing?"

She ignored him. Her head was raised, her eyes closed, and she was singing as she had not sung for more than four years. It was the song of rejoicing at the laying of a new warm egg.

"Tarkah, tarkah, tark!"

"Semolina!" He got out of bed, intending to lift her back into the basket, but then the noise started outside the win-

dow, the same egg song echoing through the darkness. He pressed his face against the window. The rain had stopped, and the sky was as black as a cave. No light at all. Yet from every chicken barn came the same sound from hundreds of voices. The egg song gathered strength until it seemed to fill every space on the farm and then some. It was like a hundred choirs singing the same notes over and over.

"Tarkah, tarkah, tark. Tarkah, tarkah, tark."

What was happening? Chickens never laid eggs at night! It must be the fox! he thought. This was a warning of some kind!

Except that Semolina didn't look scared. Her beak was open, her throat was quivering and the screens of her eyelids were closed as though she was watching something inside her head.

Josh heard feet on the boards above his head. His father was awake and running down the stairs, and the phone in the kitchen was ringing.

The chicken noise grew louder until the air inside and outside the house was quivering with egg song. Josh put Semolina back in the basket, but she didn't stop singing. The

sound drilled right through his head. He opened his door and saw his father in the hall.

Tucker was pulling his pants on over his pajamas, and he was crying, big sobs that were halfway to laughter. "Josh, you got a baby sister, born six minutes ago, and they're fine! They're both grand as can be!"

Chapter Ten

LATER THAT MORNING, JOSH put his photo card, *The Story of the Little Red Hen*, on the wall. He decided he would make a similar card for baby Tori, pictures of her family, the house, the farm, Grandma, Semolina, and on top of the card he would write, *On the night you were born, three thousand and one chickens sang you their egg song.*

• • •

Tori looked like a sleeping doll rolled up in a blanket. Josh hadn't expected her to be so small, even though Elizabeth told him that six-and-a-half pounds was a reasonable size for a baby. The other surprise was all her hair. The only other new baby Josh had seen up close had been bald. Tori had black hair that stood up on her head like a rooster's comb, and above her closed eyes were two sketchy black eyebrows as fine as feathers. Her nose was small and pointed, and her mouth folded up as though it hadn't been used yet.

"Do you want to hold her?" Tucker asked.

He hesitated.

Elizabeth smiled. "She may have come four weeks early, but she's very strong."

He held his arms out and his mother put the baby against him, showing him how to place his hands, one under her neck to steady her head. Tori didn't open her eyes, but she snuffled a bit. He stared at her. She'd grown for eight and a bit months and then come out of his mother's round belly

like a chick coming out of an egg. But she was more helpless than a baby chicken. He might have to wait awhile before he showed her his boat and Semolina and the rainbows over the chard patch.

Tucker always said that news went around the county quicker than a head cold, and within three days it was like all the folk in the area were singing egg songs too. The phone rang and rang, and there were flowers and packages for the baby and ladies from the church bringing cakes and pot roast to help Grandma out. Annalee came over with her old doll carriage.

"Don't you want to keep it?" Josh said.

"Nope. I need the space in my room. There's a teddy bear too and Jumbo the gray velvet elephant. How's Semolina?"

"Getting better and better. I took off the wool coat. She—" He was going to say she said it was too hot, but he stopped himself. "She's more comfortable without it, and she's eating real good. Want to see her?"

They sat on the porch swing, Semolina crouched between

them. The old bird had a fringe of feathers top and bottom and bare skin mottled pink and white in the middle. The bite marks had closed up and were near enough to healed. Annalee laughed. "Beg pardon, Semolina, but you look as though you're wearing a bikini."

"She won't take offense," said Josh. "She doesn't know what a bikini is." He caught Annalee's quick look. Darn! He'd come paper-thin close to breaking his promise. He said quickly, "She can walk fine and stretch out her wings. Here, Semolina, climb on my knee."

The chicken took not one scrap of notice but sidled closer to Annalee, who automatically started stroking her with those long pink nails. After a while, Annalee said, "It's been a great summer."

"Not over yet."

"Soon. I go back to school end of next week."

"No!" He could not believe that the time had gone. He too would be back at school in two weeks. "You coming over the day they get home?"

She slowly stroked the back of Semolina's head with her forefinger, and Josh thought of his mother running her hands through his hair. Just watching Annalee made him want to close his eyes.

"Of course," Annalee said. "Your grandma invited us for lunch to celebrate, and I want to hold Tori. You held Tori yet, Josh?"

"Yep. I done that."

"What does she feel like?"

He tried to estimate Tori's weight. "Like about three dozen eggs."

"Josh! That's not what I meant. How is it to hold your own baby sister?"

He bent his arm to remember the little thing that had rested in it. "Really neat, I guess. Lots of hair."

"I remember when Harrison was born. He yelled a lot. He's coming for lunch too, and Bob."

"Bob's coming to see Tori?"

Annalee smiled. "No. He wants to see the chicken that stole the silver ring. He also heard you'd be launching the boat in the afternoon. He said he wants first ride."

Josh was silent. His father had suggested they launch the boat on the coming-home day. It was all planned. Mom and

Tori in the front of the car, Josh and Grandma in the back, brand-spanking-new boat on the trailer, out on the road, down the Binochettes' drive and over the cow farm, Annalee and maybe Harrison opening gates for them all the way to the river. He hadn't put Bob in that picture.

Annalee looked at him. "I told Bob I was having first ride."

He grinned. "I already got first ride reserved for Annalee Binochette!"

"That's how it should be," she said. "Isn't it called a maiden voyage?"

They both laughed a warm lazy laugh that fell on the porch like warm syrup. Josh put his hands above his head and stretched. It had been a good summer, he thought, a great summer, and it still wasn't over.

Semolina tried to get on Annalee's lap, but her claws were sharp and Annalee put her back on the swing seat. The old hen was annoyed. She pecked Annalee's hand.

"Ouch! Why did she do that?"

Josh frowned at Semolina. "She's still jittery," he said.

Annalee sucked her hand. "Did your father tell you they caught the fox?"

"They did?"

"Out by Loon Lake."

Josh glanced at Semolina, who had become very still and bright-eyed.

"Are they going to send it away to that wild animal sanctuary?" he asked.

"They can't, Josh. Someone shot it dead."

"Dang!" Josh thought he should be glad, but he wasn't. It was just a fox doing what foxes did, and if that was wrong for people and chickens, it was right for foxes. Now its life was gone. But he wouldn't allow that fact to turn into a worry wrinkle. No, sir!

Semolina jumped down off the swing and shook what was left of her feathers. Then, walking with high steps so that the silver ring jiggled and tinkled, she went across the porch, down the steps and along the path to the flower garden, where she began to scratch for worms.

Grandma was upstairs getting her room ready for the baby. She called down to him to bring up the doll carriage and toys.

"This is Tori's room when I go back home," she said.

"I'll miss you, Grandma," Josh said. "I'll be sad to see you go."

"Nonsense!" she said. "Don't talk tripe."

"I will," he insisted, and it was true. He pushed the carriage into the corner of the room and then handed her the green knitted coat. "Semolina doesn't need it anymore. It'll still be all right for Tori if it's washed."

"What?" She threw up her hands. "You trying to give your baby sister the chicken pox?"

His mouth opened. He was going to tell her that chickens didn't get chicken pox when he saw the glint in her spectacles and realized she'd made a joke. He laughed, and before he could think about it, his arms were around her. She was thick around the middle and his hands didn't meet, but all the same, he gave her a squeezy hug and then ran out of the room before she could say anything.

The next time he saw the green jacket it was washed and in the doll's carriage, on Jumbo the gray velvet elephant.

. . .

Grandma fancied up the house real nice for the luncheon. Josh helped her clean the windows and polish the oak floors with rags wrapped around the broom. They carried the crib up from the basement. It sat waiting by Elizabeth's side of the bed.

When Tucker drove up with Elizabeth and Tori, there were red geraniums and yellow daisies on the porch, and

Grandma and Josh called out, "Welcome home," as they got out of the car. Josh thought his mother looked fine and strong. Both she and his father had faces shining as though they'd eaten Tarkah's fire egg for breakfast. Tori, wrapped in the white shawl Grandma had knitted for Josh ten years ago, was asleep, eyes scrunched shut. Elizabeth took her upstairs to put her down in her crib.

Later, more people would come for the luncheon, Mr. and Mrs. Binochette, Annalee, Harrison and Bob, the Sorensons, the Sampsons, Mrs. Waters. But right now was the quiet time for Elizabeth to sit back in her own armchair in her own home and be with her family. Grandma brought in a jug of iced tea for the ladies and three bottles of her brew for the gentlemen. Mr. Binochette and Mr. Sampson said they would have iced tea, thank you very much, but Tucker smiled at Grandma and said, well, now, he'd have a brew to celebrate the day.

Elizabeth said she'd just have water because it was very thirsty work feeding a baby.

After that, they said very little, as though it was enough to enjoy being together. Semolina stayed out on the porch,

not too bothered by the changes in the day. She didn't even come into the conversation except for Josh mentioning that maybe they could get some fertile eggs for her to sit on when she next grew clucky.

"Nice idea," said Mr. Binochette.

"Let's do that!" said Elizabeth. "Semolina would love some chicks."

"Ah, maybe not," said Tucker. "Josh, chickens get clucky when a patch of skin gets itchy. Brood patch, they call it. Only thing stops the itch is sitting on eggs and keeping them warm till they hatch."

"Semolina's not too old to do that," Josh said.

"Old ain't the point, son." Tucker took a sip of the brew. "Point is she don't have too many feathers to fluff over eggs right now. Wait till they grow again and then we'll see."

Josh sat on the arm of his mother's chair. "You coming to the river this afternoon?" he asked her.

She put her arm around him. "I wouldn't miss it for anything. Tori and I will probably stay in the car and just watch, if you don't mind."

"I promised Annalee the first ride," he said.

"Well, now, I remember you told me that!" she said. "Excellent. Do you both have life vests?"

He laughed. "Sure, Mom, but don't you worry. My boat isn't the *Titanic*."

"No icebergs on Grayhawk River," said Mr. Sampson.

In the middle of a smile, Elizabeth put her head on one side and half rose out of the chair. "Hear something?"

Josh couldn't hear a thing except the water heater in the kitchen.

"Tori's awake," she said.

Grandma, Tucker and Josh followed Elizabeth upstairs and sat on the bed as she changed the baby. Tori was really good at feeding, as hungry as a little calf. Her eyes were wide open, dark, searching their faces as they talked to her.

"She doesn't take after Tucker and Josh," Grandma said.

Elizabeth smiled. "No, Mother. I think she looks a lot like you."

Grandma waved the comment away. "Don't put that on the poor little critter!" But Josh could tell she was pleased.

He followed his father downstairs while his mother and grandmother put the baby back in the crib.

"This Christmas," said Tucker, "our Christmas cards will be from Tucker and Elizabeth and family."

"And when she's big," said Josh, "I'm going to take her fishing."

There wasn't space to say more because at the foot of the stairs, Tucker let out a yell like he'd trodden on a snake. "That blessed varmint! Garn! Get out of it!"

Josh knew before he looked. Tucker had left his glass on the floor beside his chair, and Semolina was drinking the last of his brew.

"Sorry," said Mrs. Binochette. "We were talking. We didn't notice."

The noise brought Grandma and Elizabeth down the stairs.

Tucker waved at them. "Come and see this! Crazy old bird's drunk my ale. Look at her! She can scarce walk."

It was true. Semolina was mighty unsteady on her feet, and her wings were drooping near to the ground. But she was as sassy as ever, coming back to the glass for the last few drops of brown water.

Tucker turned to Josh. "You did tell me—" He stopped and scratched his head. He was trying to figure it all out.

"She couldn't have drunk a whole glass," said Elizabeth.

"She bug-spittin' could!" said Josh. He picked up Semolina and held her in front of him. "You've really messed up this time!" he scolded.

Semolina pushed her head forward until her beak was almost on his nose. "Yeah, yeah," she said in a loud voice. "So what are you going to do about it?"